FATAL INHERITANCE

Other titles available from the *Taggart* series:

Fatal Inheritance

Peter Cave

MAINSTREAM
PUBLISHING

EDINBURGH AND LONDON

From the series written by Glenn Chandler
Producer: Robert Love
Director: Alan Macmillan

First published in Great Britain in 1994 by
MAINSTREAM PUBLISHING COMPANY (EDINBURGH) LTD
7 Albany Street
Edinburgh EH1 3UG

ISBN 1 85158 628 8

A catalogue record for this book is available from
the British Library

Typeset in Garamond by Pioneer Associates, Perthshire
Printed in Great Britain by
B.P.C. Paperbacks Ltd, Aylesbury, Bucks.

For the staff and regulars of
The Back Beyond Saloon, Killington,
Vermont, USA

Prologue

Even with the wipers slashing across the car windscreen at double speed, and the headlights on full beam, Caroline was driving more by instinct than by sight, for it was almost impossible to see more than a few yards ahead.

It was another foul night, following a week of torrential rain and high winds which had swept across most of Scotland and the North of England. The weather had caused severe problems even on the motorways and major traffic routes, but it was on the smaller back-roads that the damage was most severe. The narrow, twisting country lane was a potential death-trap of ruts, rain-filled potholes, mud-slicks and pieces of broken branches. Flanked on both sides by heavy woodland, an almost unbroken wall of dense trees overhung the single-track road, effectively blanketing out any brief glimmers of moonlight which managed to penetrate the thick layer of storm cloud.

Yet despite all this, Caroline drove at reckless speed, gunning the powerful BMW around the tight curves and through the potholes and puddles like one possessed. And perhaps a form of possession was exactly what it was. The possession of youth, of innate trust in her knowledge of the road, her driving ability, and the false sense of immortality which only the young hold.

There was another reason for her haste, of course. Perhaps the enticing lure of infatuation, the excitement of illicit romance. Certainly it was not love. Even in her moments of highest passion, Caroline never deluded herself that she was in love with Gerald Napier. Although she was only twenty-two, she was worldly-wise enough to know the difference. There had been casual boyfriends with whom sex had been more of an obligation than a pleasure, and there had been lovers who had stirred her to violent, if temporary, bursts of sexual frenzy. But never a real *affair*. And her relationship with Gerald Napier was definitely an affair, Caroline reflected. Although the actual sex was nothing to write home about, she was emotionally and physically involved with the man on several complex and binding levels. For a start, he was an older man – which in itself lent a special allure to the relationship. On top of that, he happened to be a *married* older man, which made it all the more appealing. Indeed, the fact that it was Gerald's own daughter who, as her friend, had first brought them together, gave Caroline an oddly perverse thrill.

The first rumblings of thunder rolled across the dark sky, presaging a full-scale storm. Strangely, Caroline found herself welcoming it, knowing that her journey was nearly over and she would soon be warm, dry and safe in Gerald's arms. The storm would be their ally, ensuring that they could spend the entire night together instead of a hurried, furtive coupling with their eyes on the clock. His wife, Janet, was unlikely to venture out from the cottage in such weather and Gerald would have a perfect excuse to stay overnight at the clinic. It would be the first full night they had enjoyed together since the weekend of the medical seminar in Edinburgh, two months previously.

Caroline slowed down slightly as the car passed the little country pub where they had spent several pleasant evenings together. She was now approaching the turn-off to the private drive of the Napier Health Resort and the lane narrowed even more from this point. A sudden flash of lightning cleaved the sky as she turned the steering wheel, temporarily dazzling her. She was still going much too fast. Losing her concentration for a second, Caroline felt a brief moment of panic as the car skidded on a patch of mud and loose gravel, sliding right across the drive until the offside wheels bounced over the grass verge at the side. In struggling to regain control, Caroline completely failed to see the bizarre sight which might have given her some warning of the horror which was to come.

For in the middle of the drive, positioned so that it could only have been placed there deliberately, sat a chocolate-coloured life-sized baby doll. It could have been a sentinel, or a totem of warning – but it was a warning which Caroline missed. The BMW's wheels rolled past the doll as its glass eyes flashed a fiery reflection of the next lightning streak.

The large metal gates sealing off the private grounds and gardens of the health resort came into view. They were closed. Caroline muttered a faint and most unlady-like curse beneath her breath and brought the car to a skidding halt. She was going to have to get out and open them herself. For all the money it made, the Napier Health Resort had yet to invest in an automatic system. Opening the car door, Caroline pulled the collar of her white mac up around her neck and pushed herself out of the warm cocoon of the car into the driving rain.

She ran down the beam of the car's headlights to the gates, oblivious to the puddles beneath her expensively shod feet. Her beautifully manicured fingernails scraped harshly against the rusted metal of the heavy wrought-iron latch as she struggled to open it. The fixture stubbornly refused to pull free. With a rising sense of anger and frustration, Caroline hammered against the recalcitrant lock with the heels of her hands until the whole gate assembly rattled. The noise masked out the faint sound of rustling in the bushes at the side of the drive behind her.

Obsessed with her immediate problem, Caroline was unaware of the anorak-clad figure moving stealthily towards the front of the car, or of the headlights glinting off the shining steel blade of a particularly vicious-looking and curiously shaped knife.

The latch finally came free. With a sense of relief, Caroline pushed against the gates, which began to open with a metallic creak.

The sound ceased abruptly, as Caroline's upper torso stiffened, then arched with a brief moment of intense agony. Then the pain was gone, along with all other feeling. The hinged gate slipped away from her numb and lifeless fingertips as Caroline fell where she had been standing, to lay face down with the evil knife buried between her shoulderblades.

Her body twitched spasmodically a couple of times, and then was still. For a few moments, the falling rain splashed a small dark pool of blood into red and pink patterns against the white back of her raincoat, then finally washed it away completely.

There was never a moment's doubt in Taggart's mind as to the identity of the killer. Perhaps uncharacteristically, he regarded the murder of Caroline Kemp as an open and shut case from the word go. The entire investigation took less than two weeks, an early breakthrough being the discovery that Gerald Napier's adultery had been made known to his wife only a few days previously, via the contents of an anonymous letter.

It was more than sufficient motive for murder. And, in terms of historical precedent, one of the more frequently recurring standards: 'Hell hath no fury like a woman scorned'. Although Taggart might not have actually coined the phrase, he had used it enough to establish some sort of claim to copyright.

There was the minor problem with the murder weapon, of course. Or rather the lack of one. Despite a thorough search of the woodlands and countryside surrounding the health clinic, no trace of a knife was ever found. It would have tightened up the case to have the weapon, and any corroborating fingerprints, but in the end it didn't seem to matter. Dr Janet Napier had the motive, the opportunity and no alibi for the night other than her insistence that she had been alone in the family cottage less than three miles from the murder scene. She also had medical knowledge, which helped to explain how Caroline had been killed with a single knife-thrust which had entered in just the right place to slice between muscle and bone and pierce the heart. It was all purely circumstantial evidence, but Taggart thought it was enough to close the case.

Ten days after the discovery of Caroline's body, Taggart made the formal arrest. Flanked by Detective Sergeant Jardine and DC Jackie Reid, he squared up to Janet Napier in her private consulting room, his face composed into the impassive mask he reserved for such occasions.

'I'm detaining you, Dr Janet Napier, under Section Two of the Criminal Justice Scotland Act 1980, because I suspect you of having committed an offence punishable by imprisonment, namely the murder of Miss Caroline Kemp.'

Taggart paused briefly, glancing at the woman's face to detect the faintest flicker of emotion, but there was none. She wasn't even looking at him, merely staring blankly across the room towards the window.

Taggart sighed, revealing the merest hint of disappointment. A confession at this stage might have been nice. Taking a slow, deep breath, he relaunched himself into the standard statement. 'You'll be detained to enable further investigation into the offence to be carried out.

You are not obliged to answer any more questions but if you do say anything it may be recorded and used in evidence.'

He finished the speech and took a couple of steps back as Jardine and Jackie Reid each took hold of one of Janet Napier's arms and began to lead her away to the waiting police car outside. Taggart's head drooped as he fell into line behind them, trudging in their wake. He suddenly felt very, very weary, although it was really nothing to do with this case in particular. It was more of a cumulative thing, another few pounds of burden to the debilitating weight he seemed to have been labouring under for the past three months.

The really stupid thing was that he was aware of what was happening to him but still totally unable to do anything about it. He had observed enough signs of stress in other people to recognise it in himself, and common sense told him the answer was to ease up. But instead he fought back by throwing himself even more deeply into his work, as if that was an answer in itself.

Sooner or later, something had to give.

Chapter One

Dr Gerald Napier lolled back in the plush softness of the settee, his position suggesting relaxation. Yet fine, almost imperceptible body movements gave the lie to this apparent sense of ease, betraying a state of inner tension. His eyes strayed nervously to his watch, checking the time, before reaching for the television remote-control panel on the arm of the settee.

Again, there was a strange dichotomy apparent underneath this outwardly simple act as his thumb hovered, uncertainly, over the standby button. Part of him desperately needed to know, and to care. The other part wanted to reject it all, reject even the most casual interest in his wife's fate. He had been torn like this ever since Janet's arrest, and his detachment had been forced upon him by the actual trial. To have made the effort of going back to the court after his own part as a witness was finished would have been too much. An admission of continued concern, even actual involvement.

So he had stayed away, and tried to push it all from his mind as if it wasn't really happening. Until he started feeling a sense of guilt for rejecting his wife when she most needed his support. And now even deciding whether or not to watch the evening news caused him agonies of indecision.

It was eventually almost on impulse that Napier thumbed the button, tensing as he did so, and the TV screen flickered into life. As he had fully expected, his wife's trial was the main news story again, as it had been for the past three months.

The television company had obviously considered that the case still merited the expense of an outside broadcast unit, rather than a simple studio report. The female reporter stood, microphone poised, outside the front entrance to the Glasgow High Court, her face calm but unsmiling. 'The trial of Dr Janet Napier for the murder of beautician Caroline Kemp at the Napier Health Resort, on the 23rd of December last year, was expected to end this afternoon.'

The reporter paused for effect, whilst the camera-man panned around the small crowd of people milling about – most of them actually attracted by the presence of the OB unit than by genuine interest in the outcome of the trial. Napier sighed, involuntarily. So it was not over yet. He had been expecting a verdict – a final end to the waiting, and wondering.

'However, the jury have been out all afternoon,

clearly unable to reach a unanimous decision,' the reporter went on. 'They will now retire for the night to a city hotel, and will hopefully deliver a verdict when the court reconvenes in the morning.'

The reporter was obviously ill at ease, uncomfortably aware that all she had to offer her viewers was an anti-climax, a non-event. To fill in camera time, and to justify her own position, she began to recap on the background to the trial. 'The evidence against Dr Napier throughout the trial has been largely circumstantial, with the absence of the murder weapon a factor that must surely have weighed heavily on the minds of the jurors . . .'

Napier switched the TV off again, reaching out towards the nearby coffee table to pick up the hardback book which was lying on top of it. He turned it over, staring at the photograph of his wife on the back cover with a faintly sad smile on his lips. Flipping it over, he scanned the title: *The Lethbridge Diet – by Janet Lethbridge, MB, ChB.*

It had been her deliberate choice to write the book under her maiden name, even though the publishers had been at great pains to point out that a direct connection with the well-known Napier Health Resort would have boosted sales. Gerald Napier smiled thinly, remembering how insistent Janet had been about it, and knowing, if not fully understanding, her reasoning. Even now, after twenty years, she still felt that compulsion to give her name respectability again – to justify that for which she could not atone.

The drawing-room door sighed open behind him. Napier dropped the book on to the settee beside him and craned his neck round to identify his visitor. Belinda Napier closed the door behind her and walked slowly over towards him. Her face was an impassive mask – partly genuine ignorance and partly a feigned disinterest. She moved to the back of the settee, reaching over it to drape her arm over her father's shoulder and press her face against the side of his head.

'Well?' she murmured. 'What happened? I missed the news.'

Napier took her hand, pressing the back of it against his lips. The simple gesture betrayed the close bond between them, the true depth of their relationship. It had always been so, ever since she was born. Janet had seemed somehow disappointed in producing a girl, whilst he had adored Belinda from the second he set eyes on her. When their son Jeremy was born, three years later, the positions were reversed. Janet bonded strongly with her new son, whilst Gerald was by then totally besotted with his beautiful daughter. It set a pattern for their family life which was never to change.

Comforted by her love and the warmth of the physical contact between them, Napier forced a weak smile for his daughter's benefit. 'The jury couldn't reach a decision. I expect we'll know tomorrow.'

Belinda nodded, kissing the top of his head. 'Poor Daddy. These last few months must have been hell for you.'

Her eyes fell upon her mother's book, which had fallen open at the inscription page. Belinda read it again with a familiar sense of irony: 'To my darling husband. For all your support'.

The book had been completed and published several months before Janet had discovered her husband's infidelity, and before the murder. The message had possibly been genuine then – although it did not lessen the sense of incongruity now.

Belinda bent over the back of the settee to pick up the book, snapping it shut and wishing that she could do the same with the whole, horrible business.

The crowd of reporters and photographers outside the main entrance to the High Court moved and jostled against each other like a pack of starving hyenas. There was an excited, almost desperate buzz in the air, as if the media people realised that this was their final chance to squeeze the last drop of sensationalism from the case. After this, they would all have to go back to work again, and find another personal human tragedy which could be whipped up into a matter of national importance.

At long last, Janet Napier appeared in the huge doorway at the top of the stone steps, flanked by her legal counsel and court officials. She looked out over the heads of the milling crowds as though she wasn't really seeing them, and hardly even blinked as a whole barrage of flashguns exploded in front of her eyes. For a newly freed woman, her face bore no trace of joy, even of relief. She seemed totally bemused by everything and everyone around her – much as she had looked throughout the trial.

A reporter from the *Evening Times* managed to force his way through the rest of the crowd, pushing himself aggressively up the steps and thrusting a micro-phone under Janet's nose. 'Dr Napier – how does it feel to have a "Not Proven" verdict found against you?' he demanded.

Janet chose to ignore him, instead addressing the whole crowd as though she needed to say something to the entire world. 'I just have a very simple statement to make,' she said in a surprisingly calm but strong voice. 'I did not kill anyone. That is all.'

She began to walk down the steps, even as the reporters pressed in around her, increasingly conscious that their prey was about to escape them. Two court officials fought to hold back the milling throng as she managed to reach the pavement. With their assistance, she was able to struggle to the waiting car where her son Jeremy held the door open and fought his own battle to keep a haven of space around him.

In a matter of seconds, Janet Napier was in the car and the door had been slammed shut with the child locks down and the windows fully wound up. She sat rock-still, not glancing to her left or her right as Jeremy jumped into the driving seat and began to move away. Then she was gone, leaving the crowd of frustrated and hyped-up media hyenas thirsting for blood and another victim.

It was unfortunate that Detective Chief Inspector Jim Taggart chose that precise moment to make his exit from the courthouse, stamping out through the door with Mike Jardine keeping a wary distance behind him. Jardine had seen his chief in one of these black moods before, and had learned from experience to stay well behind the line of fire.

Taggart halted at the top of the courthouse steps, looking much like the proverbial stag at bay. He regarded the baying pack of newshounds with a glowering, malevolent stare. 'And I've got absolutely nothing to say,' he growled at them, taking a certain perverse pleasure at their obvious disappointment.

It did not, however, improve his mood. He was still fuming with frustration as he stormed through the entrance and foyer of Maryhill Police Station and headed for his inner sanctum. DC Jackie Reid glanced up from her desk as Taggart strode past. Her eyes caught those of Mike Jardine, and flashed an unspoken question. His almost imperceptible, but still very definite, shake of the head gave her the answer she was looking for. It was not a good time to say anything to Taggart, not even offer condolences.

Taggart pushed through to his private office and threw himself down on the chair by his desk. Jardine hovered by the door uncertainly, not sure whether to stay around or make a discreet exit. He stared at Taggart awkwardly, feeling the urge to offer some sort of comfort but somewhat unsure of the response it might evoke.

Finally, his mere presence served as an escape valve for Taggart's pent-up anger and frustration. Glancing up at his colleague, he slammed his clenched fist down on the desk top. 'Not proven!' Taggart spat out, as if still unable to believe the verdict. 'Was that jury deaf and blind as well as stupid? She had the motive, the opportunity, and she had guile.'

'But no murder weapon,' Jardine reminded him as gently as he could. 'We always knew that was likely to be one of our weak points.'

Taggart shot him a dismissive frown, unwilling to let himself off the hook of his own guilt by accepting the obvious sop. 'Dammit – that health farm is surrounded by woods and rivers and fields. She disposed of it somewhere – we just didn't look hard enough.'

There wasn't much else Jardine could say. He could understand his chief's frustration at having lost an important case, although the sheer intensity of Taggart's reaction was slightly surprising. They had lost cases before, but this one seemed different somehow. Perhaps it was the 'Not Proven' verdict, he thought. To all intents and purposes it could be seen as a conviction – but one where the guilty party still managed to walk free. After all the work involved in putting a case together and preparing it for trial, to be so near and yet so far, must be particularly frustrating.

The telephone shrilled somewhere in the outer office. Seconds later, Jackie Reid poked her head around the portal of Taggart's office door. She looked apologetic.

'And I don't want any sympathy from you, either,' Taggart barked at her before she could open her mouth.

The young DC was clearly taken aback. Even though she was used to Taggart's bluff manner, he was rarely openly rude like this. Her normally smiling face hardened into an expression of cold efficiency. 'It's your wife, sir. She's on the phone,' she announced flatly.

Taggart frowned, snatching up the receiver on his desk and gripping it as though he wanted to throttle the thing. 'Aw, Jean – what is it?' he demanded. 'How can you bother me at a time like this?' He paused for a few seconds to listen to what she had to say. As she spoke, the scowl on his face melted into an expression of shocked disbelief. 'You're calling me *now* to ask me about the kitchen ceiling? Jean, do you not realise I've just lost an important case? I don't care a damn about the kitchen ceiling.' He seemed about to slam the phone down again when he suddenly changed his mind. His expression and tone softened slightly. 'Look, I'm sorry. I said I'd sort it out and I will. I'll speak to the builder this afternoon, all right?'

He dropped the receiver back into its cradle, looking up at Jardine with a plea for understanding in his eyes. 'Women! They think all you have time to do is worry about shades of paint.'

He jumped up from his desk, strode across the office and pushed his way past Jardine into the corridor. He walked straight into the path of DC Campbell, who was just carrying a cup of coffee back to his desk. A collision was unavoidable. Taggart's voice rose to an angry scream as the hot liquid splashed over his suit and the neck of his shirt. 'Are you stupid or something? Could you not see me? I'm big enough!'

His explosion of anger echoed along the corridor and into the outer office, causing a minor ripple of shockwaves. Typewriters suddenly ceased clacking, conversations died, heads lifted and turned in Taggart's direction.

It also brought Superintendent McVitie out from his inner sanctum, to find out what all the fuss was about. Identifying Taggart as the eye of this particular storm, he barked out an order. 'Jim – my office, please.'

Taggart hesitated for a moment, then complied. Meekly, he trotted along the corridor and allowed McVitie to usher him into his office. He stood at the side of the desk as his superior closed the door firmly.

McVitie walked to his desk and sat down, looking up at Taggart with a stern, yet somehow sympathetic, expression. 'Sit down, Jim. We need to talk.'

Taggart looked sulky. 'I'd rather stand,' he muttered petulantly. 'If it's all the same to you, sir.'

McVitie's expression did not change, but his eyes moved rather pointedly to the chair in front of his desk. It was not all the same to him, the simple gesture said. Taggart got the message loud and clear. He pulled the chair across and sat himself down, staring across the desk at his superior's face.

'We have to accept a jury's verdict,' McVitie said quietly, after a brief pause.

Taggart grunted. 'Well, *you* accept it, then,' he muttered bitterly. 'In the meantime I'll just go back out there and carry on arresting innocent people.'

'The jury *didn't* find her innocent,' McVitie reminded him.

It was supposed to reassure, but served only to evoke a careless shrug of Taggart's shoulders. 'Same thing – she walks free,' he observed.

McVitie sighed deeply, seeing how things were. He was silent for some time, finally speaking again only when he seemed to have come to a decision about something. 'Jim, I'm ordering you to take some time off. No arguments. You've been under a lot of stress lately, and it's beginning to show.'

Taggart regarded him with disbelief. 'Are you saying I can't handle my job, sir? You think I'm cracking up, is that it?'

McVitie affected a look of exaggerated patience.

'I'm saying that maybe you're letting the job handle you, Jim. You've been working weekends, coming in on your days off. It's not good. You deserve – and you need – some time off away from it all.'

Taggart was unconvinced. He regarded McVitie with a slightly mocking expression of scepticism. 'Now, what am I supposed to do with time off?'

McVitie shrugged. 'Perhaps take Jean away for a break somewhere. Go for long walks in the countryside. Read a few good books. Look at nature.'

Now Taggart was openly sarcastic. 'In February?'

McVitie's limited fund of patience was being sorely tried, but he'd made his mind up and he was not going to be deflected from his decision, with or without Taggart's co-operation. 'The month doesn't matter. You do,' he said firmly, and with finality.

There didn't appear to be much room for manoeuvre, but Taggart tried anyway. 'And this is an order, is it?'

McVitie nodded. 'It's an order.'

Taggart's face was a study in resigned misery. Far from looking like a man who was being sent on holiday, he bore the expression of someone sentenced to ninety-nine years on a chain gang. With a final, dejected nod of his head, he rose slowly from his chair and headed for the door.

'Just remember, Jim,' McVitie called after him. 'Sometimes you win cases, sometimes you lose them. You have to learn to be philosophical about that.'

Taggart failed to take any comfort from this thought. Philosophy had never been one of his strong points. He left McVitie's office without another word.

Chapter Two

Jeremy Napier brought the car to a halt outside the front entrance of the Napier Health Resort. Once a grand old stately home and country retreat, the mansion house itself had an impressive, ivy-covered gothic façade flanked by several modern but tastefully styled outbuildings, and was set in some ten to fifteen acres of grounds. On the large lawn directly in front of the house, a number of blue-tracksuited figures walked, jogged and performed various physical exercises with resigned determination. All such activities stopped for a few moments as the car door opened and Janet Napier stepped out on to the gravel drive.

Aware that all eyes were on her, but determined to make a pretence of normality, Janet turned her back on them all and began to walk stiffly into the mansion house with Jeremy covering her rear like a royal bodyguard.

A few more guests stopped in their tracks to stare after her as Janet made her way through the baronial lobby towards the grand staircase, but she continued to ignore their morbid curiosity. It was not until her daughter Belinda appeared on the landing at the top of the staircase that her composure seemed to crack slightly. Janet broke step, pausing for a moment with her hand resting on the ornate brass banister as if she feared a confrontation.

She recovered herself quickly. Taking a firm step forward, she walked briskly up the remaining stairs to greet her daughter. There was a thin, distant smile on her face, lacking real warmth. For her part, Belinda regarded her mother stonily, without even a pretence of welcome.

'So, you're back. I suppose I'd better say congratulations.' It was a flat statement, delivered more like a complaint than anything else.

There was obviously no point in retaining the forced smile, Janet realised. She allowed it to fade away, to be replaced by a look of sadness, almost despair. 'You weren't in court.' It was a simple observation, rather than a direct accusation, but it seemed to needle the girl in some way.

'I didn't really need to be, did I?' Belinda shot back. 'It was on the television and the radio just about every time I switched them on. My famous mother – star of the Sunday supplements.'

The atmosphere between mother and daughter

was rapidly degenerating from cold aloofness to open hostility. Jeremy stepped forward quickly, attempting to act as a peacemaker between them. 'Look, Mum's been through a hell of an ordeal,' he pointed out.

The reminder failed to evince any sympathy. Belinda's eyes blazed. 'We've all been through an ordeal,' she told her brother coldly. 'Especially Dad.'

The oblique reference to her husband caused Janet to frown suddenly, as if she had only just realised that he was conspicuous by his absence. Although she had not been expecting a rapturous welcome home, Janet had thought that he might at least have come out to greet her.

'Where is your father?' she asked Belinda.

'In his study,' the girl answered. With a last, almost disdainful glance at her mother, she turned her back and walked away.

Jeremy draped his arm gently around Janet's shoulder. 'Want me to come with you? Moral support, that sort of thing?'

Janet shook her head slowly. 'No, I need to see your father alone. We'll have to talk sometime. If nothing else, we still have a business to run.'

Jeremy nodded understandingly. 'All right – but I'll be in the drawing-room if you need me.' He kissed her briefly on the top of the head and walked back down the staircase.

Janet steadied herself against the top banister rail for a moment, taking in a slow, deep breath. Then, pulling herself stiffly erect, she marched directly towards Gerald's study.

He was seated at his desk with his back to the door,

checking over some papers. If he heard Janet entering the room, he showed no sign. She stopped just inside the door, looking awkward and lost. She stood there for some time, trying to think of the right words to say, but nothing came.

It was Gerald who broke the silence, eventually. 'I'm glad that it's all over,' he murmured, without turning round.

Janet began to move towards him, the faintest flicker of relief showing on her face. For those few dreadful moments, she had feared that he was going to ignore her completely. 'The public were very supportive, but it was a nightmare. The jury took two days.'

His back still to her, Gerald nodded. There was a further period of strained silence.

'They brought in a verdict of Not Proven,' Janet blurted out finally. 'It's a verdict peculiar to Scotland.'

At last, her husband turned to face her directly. 'Yes, I have lived here long enough to know that,' he pointed out.

'It means much the same as not guilty, you know.' There was a slight catch in Janet's voice as she spoke, and a plea in her eyes. Perhaps unconsciously, she was begging for his support and reassurance, but he was unable or unwilling to give it. He shook his head slowly from side to side.

'No, it means that they thought you were probably guilty, but there wasn't enough evidence.'

The words hit her like a cold shock. Hurt showed on her face first, quickly followed by an expression of the deepest despair. The jury – then her own daughter – and now her husband. No one, it seemed, believed in her innocence. Perhaps for the first time, she began to realise how a Not Proven verdict was in fact a stigma she would have to carry for the rest of her life. It was a chilling, frightening thought. It suddenly became a matter of life and death that she make at least one person believe in her again. Her eyes began to mist with tears.

'I didn't kill her, Gerald – I swear I didn't. You needed her, and I understood that. Only the courts don't see shades of grey, do they? Only black.'

Gerald averted his eyes from the desperate plea on her face. He had nothing to offer her. 'I'll be going to live at the Glasgow flat,' he announced flatly. 'I can't stay here, or live at the cottage. You understand, don't you?'

It was another body-blow, and Janet reeled under it. Somehow, she managed to drag herself across the room to an easy chair and flopped down, burying her head in her hands. 'I can't run this place without you,' she said wretchedly.

Gerald appeared unmoved. 'I've run it without you since December,' he pointed out. 'I'm sure the staff will be loyal, and you could ease up on advertising for new clients for a while. I'm sure you'll be able to manage.'

'But we built this place up together. It was our dream,' Janet said, almost sobbing.

Gerald shrugged resignedly. 'Dreams get broken,' he murmured sadly. 'Now that you're back, perhaps you can carry on as though nothing has happened. You just can't expect me to do the same.'

Behind the shine of tears, Janet's eyes were dull,

almost lifeless. A feeling of total and utter hopelessness was gradually creeping over her, numbing her both mentally and physically. She looked like a very lost and very lonely little girl, despite the maturity of her years. She desperately wanted to touch her husband, cling to him for physical comfort, but she feared that he would push her away. Instead, she could only sit where she was, her head drooping.

'I had nothing to do with Caroline's death,' she said again, in a weak little voice. 'Please believe that.'

Gerald stared at her strained face for a long time, his own features betraying the doubts and fears which continued to torment him. 'I'd like to believe that, Janet,' he muttered finally, quietly. 'But how can I ever be sure?'

The words seemed to encapsulate the gulf which had been opened between them, and which could now perhaps never be bridged again. After that, there really wasn't anything else that either of them could say which could make the slightest difference. Doubt stood like a physical barrier between them, as solid and insurmountable as the thickest and highest wall.

Gerald Napier took one last look at his wife's tear-stained face and shook his head slowly from side to side, as if there was something he had forgotten to say, failed to do. But there was nothing, of course. Miserably, he turned away from her and walked out of the room without another word.

For the first time since the nightmare had begun, Janet Napier broke down completely, and abandoned herself to a flood of tears and deep, racking sobs which seemed to rip through every part of her body. She was still crying uncontrollably when Jeremy came to find her, nearly an hour later.

Chapter Three

To the casual observer, or someone who did not understand the essential nature of the man, the scene in Taggart's living-room might have seemed like the almost perfect example of suburban domestic bliss.

Taggart himself appeared to be at perfect ease in his favourite armchair, lolling back and studying a glossy colour brochure. In the background, the radio, tuned in to Classic FM, poured out the relaxing strains of Mahler's Resurrection Symphony. Jean Taggart, as busy and mobile as ever despite the constraints of her wheelchair, glided smoothly and silently about the room, tidying flower arrangements, picking up and replacing ornaments and generally acting like a normal proud housewife.

But there were hidden tensions lurking beneath this deceptive façade. Jean glanced over at her husband, regarding him with a curious, almost suspicious, expression on her face. It was unusual to see him in such an apparently relaxed mood. Indeed, it was more than unusual, it was positively unnerving. He'd been like this for two whole days now, and the sheer incongruity of the situation was beginning to rattle her.

Things could not be allowed to just drift along in this unsatisfactory fashion, she told herself. Somehow, Jim Taggart's rare attack of domesticity needed to be channelled into more useful and productive areas. Knowing her husband as she did, subtlety or gentle hints were unlikely to achieve anything, Jean thought. Taggart was the sort of man who only really responded to the direct approach.

Jean wheeled herself over to the table in the middle of the room and made a pretence of tidying up some discarded newspapers and magazines. 'It's wonderful that you've got some time off,' she muttered, disarmingly.

Taggart grunted, not bothering to look up or give any positive sign that he was really listening.

'It means that now you'll be able to get around to doing all those little jobs in the house that you've never had time for,' Jean went on, getting straight to the punchline.

Taggart was listening, sure enough. He suddenly sat bolt upright in the chair, dropping the brochure on to his lap. He regarded his wife with a look of horror on his face. 'What?'

'I said – now you'll be able to get round to doing something about all those little jobs you've been putting off for months,' Jean repeated. 'There's the dripping tap in the bathroom, those loose hinges on the wardrobe doors . . . and it means we won't have to pay out for a decorator to come round and paint the kitchen ceiling after all.'

Taggart's look of shock faded, to be replaced by one of pained protest. His voice took on a crafty, wheedling tone. 'Aw, Jean – you know I've been ordered to take a rest. I can't be running up and down ladders. That's the last thing I need.'

It was the response she had anticipated, but Jean was adamant. 'Well, you're not going to just sit around the house under my feet all day.' she warned him. 'That's the last thing *I* need.'

Taggart picked up the brochure he had been reading, handing it across to her for her inspection. 'I'm not going to be sitting around. I was thinking of going to this place for a few days – for my health.'

Jean glanced at the glossy brochure in disbelief. 'You? Go to a health farm?'

Taggart looked shifty. 'Well, it's never too late to start looking after your body,' he muttered unconvincingly.

'And not just *any* health farm, either,' Jean put in with heavy emphasis. She had just that second noted the name of the establishment in question. The Napier Health Resort.

Taggart was on the defensive now. 'It all looked very impressive when I was there investigating the case. And it's got a very good reputation,' he protested. 'I might as well do it right if I'm going to do it at all.'

Jean regarded him uncertainly, unsure whether to believe him or not. Even if she gave him the benefit of the doubt, there was one other consideration. 'It looks very expensive,' she pointed out dubiously. 'Where's the money coming from?'

But Taggart was prepared for that one. 'I thought I'd use some of the money Aunt Hettie left us in her will.'

Jean frowned. 'I thought we'd agreed that we were going to keep that money for a cruise,' she argued.

Taggart pulled his craggy features into an expression of anguish. 'Can you really see me stuck aboard a ship? Shuffleboard and sea-sickness? And anyway, there'll be plenty left.'

Jean's heart sank. She had done it again, she told herself resignedly. She had allowed herself to lose the initiative and let him present her with a *fait accompli*. 'And when were you thinking of going to this place – for your health?' she demanded with a weary sigh.

Taggart's face registered slightly nervous relief. 'I thought this afternoon might be a good time,' he muttered.

Taggart stepped out of the taxi, unloaded his bags and looked around to take stock of his surroundings. The Napier Health Resort was a hive of early-afternoon activity. Taggart took a step backwards as a caterpillar of joggers in blue tracksuits wound past him on their way to the gymnasium. Glancing out on to the lawn, he could see a group of overweight, middle-aged ladies attempting to play netball. It all looked a bit too enthusiastic for Taggart's taste. Picking up his two bags from the drive, he headed for the comparative safety of the house.

The reception desk was manned by a pleasant-looking man Taggart had not seen before, much to his relief. He was only too well aware that he was going to encounter some antagonism sooner or later, but at least he might be able to get checked in before any trouble blew up. He walked over to the desk, reading the name tag which Ian Gowrie had pinned to his jacket lapel.

Gowrie smiled in welcome. 'Good afternoon, sir. Checking in, are we?'

Taggart nodded, saying nothing. Taking this as an affirmation, Gowrie began to fill in a guest registration form, keeping up the standard welcoming chatter as he did so. 'Your first time here, sir?'

'As a guest, yes,' Taggart admitted. He saw no point in explaining further.

'My first week too,' Gowrie confided. 'But it really is a very nice place. I'm sure you'll enjoy your stay here, Mr . . .?'

'Taggart. J. Taggart.'

Gowrie finished filling in the registration form, finally looking up again. 'Well, if you're ready, Mr Taggart, I'll show you to your room. I've given you one of the front-facing rooms, with pleasant views out over the grounds.'

He stepped out from behind the desk and began to lead the way towards the staircase. Taggart noted that there was no attempt to carry his bags for him. Obviously you started getting good healthy exercise from the moment you checked in, he thought. Picking up his bags, he trotted in Gowrie's wake.

The room was on the first floor. Gowrie threw open the door with something of a grand gesture, revealing a small but expensively furnished suite with sweeping panoramic views of the lawns and grounds outside. It was quite luxurious, in a strictly functional sort of way. Taggart found himself quite impressed, and more than a little relieved. He had been fearing something really spartan, along the lines of a monk's cloister, or perhaps one of the interview rooms at Maryhill station.

'Very nice,' he muttered. He dropped his bags down on to the plush carpet and sat himself down on the single bed, testing it with a few experimental bounces. It was a lot firmer than he cared for.

'All our beds have orthopaedic mattresses,' Gowrie informed him, as if reading his thoughts. 'Good for the spine, you know – especially after you have had a hard day doing vigorous exercise.'

Taggart digested this information stoically, trying not to make it too obvious that the mere thought of indulging in vigorous physical exercise filled him with dread.

Gowrie crossed to the built-in wardrobe opposite the bed and opened it. 'Do you need a tracksuit, Mr Taggart – or did you bring one of your own?'

Taggart looked at him blankly. 'Tracksuit?' he echoed, as if he wasn't even sure what such an animal was.

Gowrie smiled understandingly. 'Never mind. Napier's do provide one as a courtesy service. We find that the majority of our guests feel most comfortable wearing them most of the time.' He delved inside the wardrobe and pulled out one of the blue suits which Taggart had observed outside. For some reason Taggart found himself thinking of prison uniforms and had to resist the temptation to check the window for bars.

Gowrie draped the tracksuit out on the bed and prepared to leave. 'Well, I'll let you get changed and unpacked, Mr Taggart. Take your time getting settled in. But please let me know if you have any questions, or if there is anything else you require. You know where I am if you need me.'

Taggart intercepted him before he reached the door. 'There is one thing,' he muttered. 'When's dinner, by the way?'

Gowrie shot him a disapproving look, as if he had asked for a bacon sandwich in a synagogue. 'Before we even *think* about food, Mr Taggart, the nurse will have to give you a complete personal physical check-up. Then we can look at your specific requirements and the chef will design a diet which is suited to your particular personal fitness régime.'

It all sounded rather complicated, Taggart reflected. However, he thought he understood the basically simple message concealed under all the buzz-words. Obviously, they intended to starve him. 'Sounds like fun,' he grunted.

Gowrie flashed him another one of his overly-polite smiles and departed. Taggart took the man's advice and started to unpack his bags, hanging his clothes away in the wardrobe. Finally, he stripped down to his underwear and donned the blue tracksuit – albeit with a few moments of doubt. Somehow, this simple act in itself seemed to bear all the hallmarks of burning one's bridges. Completing the standard jogger's uniform with the pair of trainers he had brought with him, he paraded in front of the mirror to view the overall effect. Surprisingly, it seemed to suit him.

There was nothing left to do now but wait patiently for the promised nurse. Taggart perched himself on the edge of the bed and waited. Eventually, there was a polite knock on the door.

'Come,' Taggart barked, forgetting for the moment that he was not in his office. The door opened, and the familiar figure of Nurse Ellen Clark strode into the room. Taggart took a deep breath. The confrontation was about to begin.

Nurse Clark stopped dead in her tracks as she recognised him. She regarded him with much the same expression as one might look at the remains of a squashed hedgehog in the gutter. 'You!' she hissed, with pure venom in her voice.

Taggart forced a disarming smile on to his face. 'Hello, Nurse Clark,' he said brightly. 'Nice to see you again.'

Nurse Clark continued to glare at him with undisguised loathing. 'You've got some gall showing your face here again,' she accused bitterly. 'Don't you think you have caused enough pain and heartbreak already?'

Lesser men would have withered under the blistering attack. Even in a good mood, Nurse Clark was a formidable woman. Angry, she was a veritable dragon. To his credit, Taggart stood his ground, maintaining the disarming smile which had so far not proved terribly effective. 'I assure you that I am here purely as a guest,' he told her.

Nurse Clark was not convinced, but outwardly at least, Taggart *was* a guest and had to be treated with courtesy. Eyeing him suspiciously, she managed to draw her features into something approaching a welcome.

'Well, if you'd like to follow me, Mr Taggart, I'll take you down to the medical room for a check-over.'

Breathing a small sigh of relief, Taggart trotted along behind her. So far, it had all been a lot easier than he had feared.

There was nothing perfunctory about the medical examination. Once again, Taggart found himself impressed with the sheer professionalism of the Napier Health Resort. They certainly took themselves seriously, and there was nothing to indicate that it was in any way just a rip-off place to part overweight middle-aged ladies from their excess wealth. Perhaps less gently than he would have wished, Nurse Clark had poked, prodded and examined just about every square inch of his body, and, using what appeared to be genuine and state-of-the-art medical equipment, had submitted him to just about every possible test known to medical science.

'Right, I just need to check your blood pressure, Mr Taggart,' Nurse Clark informed him as she wrote up the last of her notes on his respiratory tests. 'If you'd like to sit down and roll up your sleeve.'

It sounded as though it was almost over, Taggart thought gratefully. He sat down in the padded chair, rolling up the sleeve of his tracksuit. Nurse Clark moved over to her desk to lay down her notes. Discreetly, using her body to shield her movements from Taggart's eyes, she pressed a small call button on the underside of the desk. Then, wheeling over the blood pressure monitor, she wrapped the inflatable rubber bandage around his arm and began pumping it up.

Above the faint hiss from the inflation bulb, Taggart did not hear the medical room door swing quietly open behind him. Summoned by Nurse Clark's emergency call, Janet Napier crept silently to the nurse's side and dismissed her with a curt nod and a flash of her eyes. Taking over, she continued to pump up the pressure pad until it evinced a small wince of discomfort from the unfortunate patient wearing it.

'That's a bit tight, isn't it?' Taggart complained, without looking round.

'It's also a bit high,' Janet Napier muttered coldly.

Recognising her voice, Taggart whirled round suddenly, to confront her stony, expressionless face. He matched it with what he fondly imagined was a look of total innocence. 'Is that bad?'

'It depends on the cause. Perhaps you were just in too much of a hurry to get here,' Janet Napier suggested, with heavy sarcasm.

So it was to be a cat and mouse game, Taggart realised. He took some comfort from this thought, relieved that Janet Napier did not appear to be openly antagonistic. Fortunately, cat and mouse was a game at which he considered himself to be particularly skilled.

'I'm here purely as a guest, Dr Napier,' he said, not really caring whether she believed him or not. 'As far as the police are concerned, the case is closed.'

'Well, that's nice to hear,' Janet said, still highly cynical. She deflated the pressure pad and removed it from his arm. 'So, you thought you'd take a little rest break, Mr Taggart. But why *this* particular health resort, I find myself wondering?'

'I liked the setting,' Taggart said blandly. He paused

for a second, staring her directly in the eye. 'Look, more than anything else, I just need to relax. It says in your brochure that some people come here to do just that.'

Janet nodded, her expression still openly dubious. 'Yes, *some* people do,' she agreed.

'They tell me I've been overdoing it lately,' Taggart added, rather overstressing his case.

Janet Napier allowed herself a short, bitter laugh. 'Oh, I'm sure you have, Chief Inspector. You've been overdoing it all right, and I think you're overdoing it now.' She finished folding up the pressure bandage and wheeled the blood pressure monitor back across the surgery. She began to walk towards the door.

'I was just doing my job, Dr Napier,' Taggart called out after her. 'Now that I'm here, I hope you'll do yours.'

Janet paused briefly in the doorway. 'You can count on it,' she promised. She walked out into the corridor, to be confronted by Gilbert Vance, the head waiter. There was a worried and angry look on his face. He nodded his head towards the medical room.

'I've just seen the guest list,' he hissed. 'What's he doing here?'

Taking the man's arm, Janet Napier led him gently down the corridor, out of Taggart's earshot. 'Chief Inspector Taggart says that he's just here for a rest, Gilbert,' she informed him icily. 'It's going to be up to us to make sure he gets one, isn't it?'

Vance smiled at her knowingly. 'Of course, Dr Napier. I understand completely.'

Chapter Four

Gerald Napier eased the Granada into his reserved parking space and climbed out, retrieving his medical bag from the rear passenger seat before closing the door and locking it. He walked across the courtyard to the entrance of his Glasgow surgery and up the short flight of stone steps to the front door.

It was already open, on the latch. Obviously Agnes, his receptionist, had got in before him as usual. Always the last to leave in the evening, and invariably at least an hour early in the mornings, Napier often wondered if she actually had any private life outside the surgery. Perhaps she even slept there without him knowing, he had sometimes thought fancifully.

Napier returned his keys to his pocket and walked

through the lobby, glancing sideways into the waiting-room as he passed. It was empty – as it had been for much of the last few days. His private practice had suffered badly during the three months he had been forced to run the health resort on his own. It would probably be a similar amount of time before he managed to build it back up again, Napier thought.

But it was not something he was prepared to worry about now, he told himself, shrugging philosophically. As it happened, he was actually slightly relieved that he had no early-morning patients to attend to. The aftermath of the trial, and the trauma of confronting his wife on her return, still weighed heavily upon him, and he was grateful for any chance to take things easy. He strolled into his consulting room, putting on a thin smile for Agnes's benefit as he passed her at the reception desk. 'Good morning, Agnes. Any messages?'

'I'll bring them in, Dr Napier.' Agnes Pollock retrieved a small pile of letters from the top of a nearby filing cabinet and followed him in to his consulting room. She stood by the door, clutching the bundle of letters tightly, as if she was somehow unwilling to hand them over.

'Mrs Wright rang,' she murmured. 'She wanted to know if she should take the brown capsules and the red capsules at the same time. And your daughter rang twice.' She paused awkwardly, still clutching the letters as though she wasn't quite sure what to do with them. Finally, she thrust them forward with a somewhat abrupt gesture. 'Oh, and here's the morning mail. Another one of those nasty letters, I'm afraid.'

Napier frowned as he took the sheaf of letters and flipped through them, quickly identifying the particular one in question. It was unmistakable, the crudely written block capitals on the envelope now sickeningly familiar. Even though he knew exactly what the envelope contained, he ripped it open and drew out the single folded sheet of paper inside.

'Same as the others?' Agnes asked, a slightly worried expression on her face.

Napier nodded grimly, scanning the blunt, anonymous message scrawled in a childish hand. WHAT DOES IT FEEL LIKE TO BE MARRIED TO A MURDERESS?

'I think it's about time you took those letters to the police,' Agnes murmured gently, with genuine concern in her voice. 'It's just not right that you should continue to be persecuted like this. Perhaps they can find out who this sick person is and put a stop to it once and for all.'

Napier sighed heavily. His receptionist was giving him sound advice, he knew. It *was* time he did something about the anonymous letters, which had been dropping through the letterboxes of his surgery, the health resort and the family cottage with relentless regularity for over ten weeks now. 'Yes, you're right, Agnes,' he agreed. 'I will do something about it, I promise.'

Agnes was not going to be put off with such a vague assurance. She regarded him with fond concern. 'There's no time like the present,' she urged gently. 'You've no appointments until after midday. It'll only take you half an hour to drive into Maryhill and see someone. The sooner you get this business out into the open, the sooner these wicked letters will stop. I'll phone through and make you an appointment if you like.'

Napier thought about it for a moment, finally making up his mind. Agnes was quite right. There *was* no time like the present – and particularly now that the trial was over and done with, the pressure and persecution of him and his family had to stop. Folding the anonymous letter carefully, he slipped it back into its envelope and transferred it to his inside jacket pocket. He glanced at Agnes, nodding his head. 'You're right, as ever, Agnes.' he told her with a faint smile. 'I'll leave you to hold the fort for a while, if you don't mind.'

He turned away, missing the look of satisfaction, almost triumph, on Agnes's face as she realised she had got her way. It betrayed more than a matronly concern. Napier had never allowed himself to even recognise, let alone think about, the depth of Nurse Pollock's devotion to him. Had he ever done so, he might have been surprised, even a trifle alarmed, by the full intensity of her feelings.

Superintendent McVitie studied the letter carefully for some time, not quite sure why Jardine had found it important enough to refer the matter to his personal attention. Perhaps Taggart's singular obsession with the Napier case was contagious, he reflected. Finally, he handed the letter back to Gerald Napier with a slightly apologetic look. 'My advice would be to try to ignore it, if you can,' he said. 'After a sensational murder trial, such things aren't uncommon, unfortunately.'

But Napier was not to be put off quite so easily. Having finally made the effort to report the matter to the police, he was not prepared to be merely fobbed off and told to ignore it. 'Is that all you have to say?' he demanded. 'Some crank finds it necessary to intrude upon the privacy of me and my family and you think I should just turn my back on it?'

McVitie sighed. 'I can understand your concern, Dr Napier,' he muttered. 'But I really don't think you need to worry about it overduly. These things are distressing and unpleasant, I know – but there is rarely any direct threat implied. Nine times out of ten, the letters simply stop of their own volition. In our experience, the type of person who does this sort of thing either tires of writing or finds another little obsession.'

'And the tenth time?' Napier demanded sarcastically. He opened his medical bag and delved into it, pulling out a whole sheaf of similar envelopes. He dropped them on to McVitie's desktop, looking at the man directly in the eye. 'I suppose you're going to tell me to ignore all these as well?'

Jardine, who up to now had been keeping discreetly in the background, stepped forward to examine the pile of letters. With a slightly apologetic glance at McVitie, he pushed himself into the conversation. 'How long have you been receiving these?' he asked Napier.

'Since just after my wife's arrest,' Napier told him. 'There have been 26 in all – every one with exactly the same message. Some were sent to my surgery, some to the health farm.'

'You mentioned your family,' Jardine recapped. 'Have your son and daughter also received these letters?'

Napier nodded. 'We've all received them. The messages are slightly differently worded, of course – but the general theme is the same, and there's no doubt that they're from the same person.'

McVitie was showing a little more interest now. He

leaned forward over his desk, riffling through the pile of envelopes. 'Why have you not brought them to our attention before now?' he asked.

Napier shrugged. 'I suppose because I assumed that they would stop once the trial was over. Obviously, I was wrong.'

McVitie considered the matter for a few moments. He was still pretty sure that the letters were the work of a harmless crank, but he had to admit that it was a little unusual for a hate campaign to go on for so long, or with such intensity. Perhaps his original assessment of the situation had been a trifle hasty, he decided. He looked across at Napier again. 'Look, I'll arrange for an officer to come round and interview the rest of the family,' he announced after a while. 'We'll collect all the letters, look into it and see what we can do, although I can't promise anything, you understand.'

For a second, a worried frown creased Gerald Napier's forehead. 'You're not thinking of sending Chief Inspector Taggart, I hope.'

McVitie noted the man's obvious concern, and could understand it. He hastened to reassure him. 'Chief Inspector Taggart is on leave for a while,' he announced firmly. 'He's currently taking a well-deserved holiday with his wife.'

It was a statement which McVitie made in all sincerity, even though it was quite wrong.

Chapter Five

Jardine and DC Jackie Reid were as impressed with the outside of the Napier Health Resort as their chief had been. Stepping out of the car, Jardine gazed across the lawns to where Ian Gowrie was putting a large bunch of guests through a series of particularly strenuous-looking exercises. It looked like hard work, Jardine thought.

He looked at Jackie, grinning. 'Would you pay hundreds of pounds a week to put yourself through that?' he asked her. 'For the same sort of money, you could probably be laying out in the sunshine by the swimming pool of some luxury hotel in the Canaries.'

Jackie was eyeing up Gowrie's superb physique with obvious appreciation. 'This place probably has its compensations,' she murmured, expressing the female viewpoint.

Jardine smiled, in a rather superior, almost smug, fashion. 'I don't think people come to health farms to do that sort of thing,' he observed.

Jackie merely grinned, shaking her head from side to side very faintly. 'You know, Michael – that's probably one of the things I find most appealing about you,' she told him. 'Your sublime innocence.'

Jardine let the jibe go. He led the way up the stone steps to the entrance.

Jeremy Napier looked slightly the worse for wear as he peered out at them from behind the half-closed drawing-room door. Still clad in his pyjamas underneath a silk dressing-gown, he regarded Jardine and Jackie Reid morosely through puffy, slightly bloodshot eyes. 'What do you two want at this time of the morning?' he demanded, somewhat aggressively.

Jardine glanced at his watch. 'It's five to eleven,' he felt obliged to point out, defensively.

Jeremy groaned. 'That's what I mean.' He glared at them for a few more seconds, as though hoping they would just go away. Finally, he seemed to accept that his morning of rest was over. 'Well, I suppose you'd better come in,' he muttered grudgingly.

He opened the drawing-room door, allowing, if not exactly inviting, them in. The room was dark, with heavy brocade curtains still closed against the weak morning sunlight. Furnished in the ornate, almost gothic style of the rest of the mansion house, the general atmosphere was gloomy, even brooding. Looking at Jeremy's ravaged features and pallid complexion, Jackie Reid had the strangest sensation of having bearded a vampire in his lair.

'I hope you don't mind if I don't open the curtains,' Jeremy muttered. 'Got a bit of a headache. Rather a late night last night.'

'Anywhere interesting?' Jardine asked, conversationally.

'Just the local pub.' Jeremy retreated to an armchair and sank down into it with another faint groan.

'You should be out with the early-morning joggers,' Jackie suggested brightly. 'It might help to clear your head.'

Jeremy looked at her as though she had just mouthed some terrible obscenity. 'The punters come here to get fit. I just like the money they bring with them,' he said, candidly.

'Is your mother around?' Jardine asked. Somehow, he got the feeling that Jeremy Napier was not going to be particularly helpful.

Jeremy shook his head, instantly regretting it as a wave of giddiness and nausea hit him. 'She's not here. She's gone up to the cottage in Perth. Mainly to get away from people like you. She'll probably be back tomorrow.'

'So who's in charge?' Jackie wanted to know.

'Belinda – but I think she's busy giving someone a seaweed wrap at the moment. She can't really be disturbed. What is it you want, anyway?'

'Actually, we need to speak to you both,' Jardine told him. 'It's about the anonymous letters you've all been receiving.'

'Oh, those.' Jeremy was totally dismissive. 'I just burn the damned things. That's all they're fit for.'

Jackie Reid tended to agree with him, but they had been sent to do a job. 'What about your sister?' she asked.

'Her too. They all say exactly the same thing – "How does it feel to have a murderess for a mother" – or something like that.' Jeremy pushed himself up out of the armchair and crossed the room to a drinks cabinet, pulling out a bottle of Glenfiddich. 'I need a drink. Either of you want one?'

Jardine answered for both of them. 'A little early in the day – even if we weren't on duty. How many?'

Jeremy poured himself a large measure of whisky with a shaking hand. 'How many what?'

'How many of these anonymous letters have you and your sister received?'

Jeremy shrugged. 'Oh, I don't know. At least a couple of dozen, I suppose. I never bothered to count them. Why give some sicko a perverse sense of satisfaction by even reading the damned things?'

'Well, if you get any more, would you keep them for us, please?' Jardine asked. 'Your father has asked us to investigate the matter, and we need to examine as many of the letters as we can. We'll check back with you in a week or so.'

Jeremy threw his drink down his throat in one gulp. 'What's the big deal, anyway? They're obviously just the work of some nut.'

'But this nut is obviously very disturbed,' Jackie Reid pointed out. 'He might not stop at just sending anonymous letters.'

Jeremy stared at her for a long moment, something approaching shock registering on his face. 'Do you really think so?' He turned to the drinks cabinet again to refill his glass.

Jardine nudged Jackie discreetly. 'Come on, I think it's time to go,' he murmured.

They walked out of the room and along the corridor. 'I'd say that young man had a bit of a problem, wouldn't you?' Jardine asked, as they reached the top of the staircase and began to descend.

But Jackie wasn't listening. She had stopped, abruptly, in mid-step, clutching the balustrade and staring down across the open reception area below. 'Mike – can you see what I see?' she whispered, incredulously.

Jardine followed her gaze. Across the foyer, it was possible to see right into part of the guest lounge, through the open double doors. And there, clad in a blue tracksuit and snoozing in a plush armchair, was a familiar figure.

'I don't believe it,' Jardine breathed. He blinked a couple of times, as if his eyes were playing tricks on him. The figure was still there. Jardine glanced sideways at Jackie, a baffled look on his face. 'I'd say this merits further investigation, wouldn't you?'

An emphatic nod from his colleague gave Jardine the answer he wanted. Together, they bounded down the remaining stairs and swept into the lounge. Jardine prodded the snoozing figure on the shoulder.

Taggart awoke with a start, looking up at first in surprise and then with a slightly guilty frown. He recovered himself quickly, adopting his more usual dour expression. 'Oh, hello,' he muttered, in a matter-of-fact tone. 'Fancy seeing you two.'

Jardine stared at him in total bewilderment. 'Sir – what are you *doing* here?' he demanded.

Taggart regarded him with a blank expression. 'Doing exactly what I was told,' he said simply. 'The Biscuit ordered me to take a rest, so I'm taking one. You can't get more restful than this.'

Jardine looked around the rest of the guest lounge. 'Where's Jean?'

Taggart assumed a look of mock horror. 'I've come away to *avoid* stress,' he said pointedly.

Jackie was looking round at the ornate surroundings. 'This place is a bit expensive for your tastes, isn't it, sir?' she put in.

'You can't put a price tag on good health,' Taggart told her smugly. 'Besides, Auntie Hettie's paying for it – or at least, her legacy is.'

Jardine was still shaking his head in disbelief. 'I suppose you do realise that The Biscuit will go bananas, don't you?' Jardine pointed out.

Taggart looked slyly secretive. 'The Biscuit doesn't have to find out, does he? Unless of course a certain two people have to blab their mouths off like a couple of girls at a hen party.' Taggart paused, suddenly realising that he had a question of his own. 'By the way – what are *you* doing here, while we're on the subject?'

Jardine told him about the anonymous letters, after briefly thinking about it and finding no valid reason why he should keep it a secret. Taggart seemed to digest the information without much apparent interest. 'Well, I suppose you'd best be getting back to the station,' he said eventually, retrieving his morning paper from where it had fallen on to the floor. 'I have some serious relaxing to do.'

Jardine and Jackie exchanged a bemused glance. 'Yes, well . . . have a good rest,' Jardine muttered uncertainly. 'And you can rely on us to be discreet, sir.'

Taggart nodded. 'I was counting on it,' he said confidently. He dropped his eyes to the newspaper and began reading it, effectively dismissing them both.

Jardine and Jackie took the hint. Still wearing slightly puzzled expressions, they left Taggart to his own devices and headed for the way out. Only when they were sure that they were safely out of the range of Taggart's acutely sensitive hearing did Jackie allow herself to voice the question which was on both their minds. 'What does he think he's up to?' she hissed at Jardine.

Jardine could only shrug, being totally lost for a plausible answer. 'The only thing I *do* know for sure is that The Biscuit is going to hit the roof if he finds out,' he told her as they reached the car.

'Not a word shall pass my lips,' Jackie vowed, and meant it. The thought of McVitie's anger, and Taggart's subsequent wrath, were too terrible even to contemplate.

In fact, it was the top of his desk that McVitie hit. Fiercely, with his clenched fist, and about three seconds flat after Jardine and Jackie Reid reported to his office as ordered. He looked like a man on the verge of apoplexy as he glared at them both. 'Get Taggart on the phone for me,' he barked at Jackie.

DC Reid feigned innocence. 'Where is he, sir – do

we know?'

McVitie shot her a withering glance. 'Are you trying to be funny, young woman?' he demanded.

'Sorry, sir.' With a slight gulp, Jackie headed for the phone.

There was obviously no point in trying to keep up the pretence any longer, Jardine realised. Somehow, the cat was well and truly out of the bag. 'How did you find out, sir?' he wanted to know, rather puzzled.

McVitie picked up a pencil from his desk and toyed with it irritably. 'Because his wife called me half an hour ago, that's *how*.' The pencil snapped in his hands. Dropping the two broken halves on to his desk, McVitie glared across at Jackie Reid again. 'Have you got hold of him yet?'

'They're trying to find him now, sir. They seem to think that he might be in the hot tub.'

Little muscles danced neurotically in McVitie's face. 'Hot tub?' he stormed. 'I'll give him more hot water than he's ever dreamed of,' he threatened darkly. 'Does he imagine for one moment that I don't know what he's doing there?'

'With respect, sir – he does say he went there to relax,' Jardine said quietly, trying to defuse the situation. He had never seen The Biscuit quite so angry.

The words failed to assuage his chief's fury. 'Relax?' McVitie spat out contemptuously. 'That man doesn't know the meaning of the word.'

'I have him now, sir,' Jackie called, holding the receiver out towards him. McVitie snatched it from her grasp with a shaking hand.

'Jim – I want you out of that place immediately,'

he yelled into the mouthpiece. 'The case is closed, and there's no more to be said about it.'

There obviously *was* something more to say, and it appeared that Taggart was saying it. McVitie was stunned into temporary silence as Taggart launched into his argument. The expression on his face passed from fury into shock, and from shock through to disbelief. Eventually, he pulled the receiver away from his ear and stared at it impotently, his mouth opening and closing like a fish out of water. Like a man in a daze, he slowly placed it back in its cradle, and gaped up at Jardine and Jackie, for the moment rendered totally speechless with indignation.

'Anything wrong, sir?' Jackie asked politely, struggling to keep a straight face.

McVitie stared at her blankly for a few seconds. 'He hung up on me,' he breathed, incredulously, at last. 'The bloody man says I'm causing him stress.'

Chapter Six

It could easily have been a macabre flashback to the
night of Caroline Kemp's grisly murder. The white BMW
jolted over the same rutted lane leading up to the Napier
Health Resort, through another storm-wracked, blustery
night. The car's blazing headlights sliced along the rain-
soaked road ahead, turning the patches of puddle water
into glistening mirrors.

Behind the wheel, Belinda Napier strained her eyes
out through the windscreen, past the hypnotic sweep of
the wipers. She was fighting to keep her full concentration on her driving, although it wasn't easy. Belinda
had never felt really comfortable driving on this back-
road, especially late at night, and now there were other
factors to nag at her mind. The murder of her friend had

left frightening doubts along with the emotional scars. If, after all, her mother had been truly innocent, could there still be a killer loose out there somewhere?

It was with a distinct feeling of relief that the great iron gates of the health resort finally came into view, but tonight they were fully opened. Thankful for this small mercy, Belinda turned into the private drive and cruised up to the front of the house. Jumping out of the car quickly, she slammed the doors and ran for the cover of the porchway, pausing there only long enough to strip off her raincoat and shake it briefly before letting herself into the house.

She crossed the lobby and began to climb the darkened stairway, not bothering to switch on the lights. Although the great house was silent as the grave, there was a certain amount of residual light showing under the bottoms of some of the guest-rooms on the first floor. It was enough to guide her way, and she was on familiar ground anyway. She passed the first landing, continuing up the stairs towards the private staff and family rooms on the second floor. Reaching the top, she crept slowly along the corridor towards her own bedroom, feeling her way along the banister rail. It was darker now, and what little light reached up to the second floor threw further long, slanting shadows into the gloom.

But the lurking figure ahead of her was not a shadow. Belinda's body stiffened, giving a little start of surprise as someone stepped suddenly out into her path, blocking her way along the corridor in a clearly deliberate manner. It was only a matter of a split second before recognition – not long enough for actual fear to quite register. Nevertheless, it was a confrontation which filled Belinda with quiet dread. She let out a heavy sigh of despair.

'It's you,' she hissed at the dark figure. 'I thought you were at the cottage.'

Janet Napier closed the five-foot gap between her and her daughter, until they stood directly facing each other. Her features were drawn into a tight mask of impassivity, suggesting that she too took no pleasure from the nocturnal meeting. 'I came back here specially tonight. I wanted to talk to you,' Janet murmured quietly.

Belinda sighed again. 'It's late. I'm tired.' She tried to push her way past, but Janet moved sideways to prevent her. She had waited for over three hours for this meeting, and she was not to be cheated now. 'Where have you been until this hour?' Janet demanded. 'You've been with your father, haven't you?'

Belinda glared at her mother, defiance blazing in her eyes. 'Yes, I have – and why shouldn't I have been? He needs someone – and who else is there for him now?'

The words carried an implication which Janet found quite chilling. Her shoulders slumped in resignation. She regarded her defiant daughter with a look of deep sadness in her eyes. 'Why have you taken his part in all this? Did it never occur to you that I might have needed support too?' Janet paused, briefly, almost afraid to voice her own fears. 'You still believe I killed her, don't you?'

It was the direct challenge which Belinda had always dreaded. The final confrontation which had been threatened ever since her mother's arrest. It was the reason why she had stayed away from the trial, refused to visit her mother in prison, tried so desperately to keep the question at a distance. Even now, she was unwilling to face it, let alone give an answer.

Belinda made another attempt to push past her mother. 'Look, I've told you I'm tired, and it's late. I don't want to talk about this now.'

Janet seized her arm, holding it in a surprisingly strong, vice-like grip. 'But I do,' she insisted, her voice rising in frustration. 'You and I have to come to terms with this thing, Belinda.'

Belinda struggled to break free. 'You're hurting my arm,' she complained. 'Why can't you just leave me alone? Leave Dad alone?'

Janet finally released her grip on her daughter's arm and took a step backwards, still blocking any further progress down the corridor. 'It was your father who started all this, not me,' she reminded Belinda in a quieter, calmer tone. 'And you helped him – remember?'

'And who could blame him?' Belinda shot back, her voice rising in anger. 'The pair of you haven't slept together for years. You never cared a damn about Dad's needs, even his work. It was always *you* – your health clinic, your books, your career. It was like you were the queen bee and he was just a drone. Dad deserved better than that.'

Janet cringed under the blistering attack – particularly stinging because she knew so much of it to be true. She was about to make a defensive plea when a door along the corridor behind her opened suddenly, and Ian Gowrie's angry voice hissed out through the darkness.

'Please, will you keep your voices down? Don't you realise what time it is?'

A light snapped on, and Gowrie stepped out on to the landing, clad in his dressing-gown. Recognising Janet and Belinda, he was at once apologetic. 'Oh, I'm sorry, Dr Napier – I didn't realise it was you. I thought it was guests wandering about, causing a disturbance.'

Janet forced a calming smile. 'It's all right, Ian. I'm sorry, it was just a private family discussion. We didn't realise we were talking so loudly.' She turned back to her daughter. 'Look, Belinda – we really do have to talk about this. Perhaps tomorrow?'

Belinda didn't answer. She had just noticed a thin shaft of light from a half-open door on the floor below. She peered over the banister rail just as the door closed with a faint click and Taggart ducked back into the safety of his room with a slightly guilty expression on his face. 'Not so private as you thought,' Belinda said to her mother. 'It seems we have an eavesdropper.'

Taggart sat at his breakfast table, irritably poking at a gooey concoction on his plate with a tablespoon. Scooping up a small amount, he sucked it tentatively between his lips. It tasted as insipid as it looked. Taggart's face screwed up into an expression of distaste. He dropped the spoon into the plate, calling over to Gilbert Vance, who was swanning proudly around the breakfast room like Charles of the Ritz.

'Excuse me, but what's this?' Taggart demanded, nodding at the stewed sludge on his plate.

Vance shot him an annoyed glance. He would have

liked to ignore the man, but he had been instructed to treat Taggart like any other guest. Reluctantly, he moved in the general direction of Taggart's table, pausing to greet a couple of female guests on the way. 'Good morning, Angela, good morning, Mrs Drake. I hope you're enjoying your stay with us this time.'

Finally, he deigned to come over to Taggart's table. He was smiling politely, but there was a vague look of contempt in his eyes. 'All settled in, are we, Mr Taggart?' he asked obsequiously. 'And what can I do for you this morning?'

Taggart jabbed his forefinger at the contents of his plate, repeating his earlier query. 'What *is* this?' Taggart wanted to append the word 'muck' to the question, but decided against it. It was implied, anyway.

Vance reeled off the contents of the stewed fruit dish like one of the judges on *Masterchef*. 'Apricots, prunes and crushed raisins, mixed with a little honey and water, then delicately baked and sprinkled with lemon rind.'

Taggart grunted. 'Aye, I thought it might be,' he muttered. 'Do I get a choice?'

Vance dashed his hopes immediately – rather eagerly, Taggart thought. 'Your personal diet programme is very specific, Mr Taggart. Dr Napier worked it out herself.'

Taggart looked crestfallen. 'That's what I was afraid of.' He glanced longingly towards the next table, where an extremely overweight woman was happily tucking into a particularly juicy-looking kipper.

Noticing his attention, she smiled at him. 'Good morning,' she said brightly.

Taggart merely nodded and forced his attention

back to the prune and apricot concoction.

The woman beckoned Vance over. 'Gilbert, this Loch Fyne kipper is superb, as usual,' she trilled.

Vance preened. 'I'm so glad, Lavinia.' He picked up a carafe of apricot juice on her table and refilled her glass for her. Lavinia smiled up at him sweetly, finishing off her kipper and holding up her plate for him to take away.

'I don't suppose there's the teensy-weensiest chance of having another one, is there?' she asked, in a coquettish, little-girl voice.

Vance gave her a conspiratorial smile. 'I don't see why not. Let me see what I can do.' Taking her plate, he trotted off towards the kitchen.

The woman returned her attention to Taggart, sliding her chair along the table and leaning over towards him. 'Your first time here, isn't it? I can always tell. I come here every year. I also go to Haggerty Castle but they starve you far more than they do here, so I only go there when I really want the calories to fall off.' She broke off to extend her hand. 'I'm Lavinia Jeffrey, by the way – but please call me Lavinia.'

Taggart shook her hand briefly. 'Taggart – Jim,' he muttered brusquely, but it was enough to open up a legitimate channel for friendly conversation.

'I'm off to Monte Carlo next week,' Lavinia informed him, as if she was letting him in on the greatest secret since the invention of fire. 'So I shall probably put most of it straight back on again within the month, but what the hell?' She paused again, to study Taggart's small and wiry frame intently. 'You certainly don't look as though you're here to lose weight.'

'No, I'm not.' Taggart would have been quite happy

to leave it at that, but Lavinia Jeffrey had other ideas. She glanced at the contents of his breakfast plate.

'I used to suffer terribly from irritable bowel syndrome,' she said candidly. 'Stewed fruit proved the answer – kept me regular as clockwork. Is it bowel problems you're having?'

Taggart shook his head. 'No, I'm just here to relax.'

Lavinia nodded knowingly. 'Ah, a businessman,' she said. 'A chance to get away from all the pressures of decision-making, the constant ringing of the telephone and all those rushed business lunches. Oh, I know what it must be like. I've met lots of businessmen here. Most of them even refuse to accept telephone calls from their wives.'

'Is that right?' Taggart muttered, trying to show polite interest. He was somewhat relieved to see Vance reappearing, bearing a silver tray on which were piled several tempting, reddish-golden kippers. Selecting the fattest, he laid it out on a fresh plate and placed it in front of Lavinia.

Taggart clutched at the man's jacket. 'Do you think I might have one of those, please?' he asked hopefully.

Vance flashed him a 'who's a naughty boy then' look. 'Now, now, Mr Taggart. We must adhere strictly to our personal diet plans, mustn't we?'

Taggart gave the man a sickly grin. 'Oh, of course we must,' he muttered sarcastically. 'Forgive me for asking – I don't know what came over me.' He stared longingly after the departing plate of kippers as Vance bore them away towards more favoured guests.

Lavinia Jeffrey misinterpreted his stare as curiosity about the other guests. Never one to miss the chance of spreading a bit of gossip, she hastened to fill him in with the details. Edging her chair even closer to his table, she leaned over to Taggart and delivered her information in an excited whisper. 'That lady on your immediate right is Mrs Drake,' she told him. 'She's a regular here too, but she keeps herself very much to herself. She has some dark secrets, that one. A bit of a mystery woman, if you ask me.'

Despite himself, Taggart felt his ear pricking with natural curiosity. 'Mystery woman?'

Lavinia nodded. 'Well, just look at her,' she hissed. 'You can't tell me that woman isn't trying to hide something.'

Taggart *did* look – as discreetly as possible, having to admit to himself that Mrs Drake was an unusual-looking woman. She was probably aged around fifty-five, but chose to disguise her age under a shock of bleached hair which looked like a wig, extremely heavy make-up and a pair of dark glasses. There was definitely something furtive about her bearing and mannerisms.

However, he was not allowed to dwell on the subject for long. Lavinia was already directing his attention to the next guest. 'Now that younger woman sitting next to her is here to dry out,' she announced. 'She drops in here for a week whenever she's been hitting the bottle too hard. Or rather, her husband puts her in, as I understand it. He's some sort of bigwig with the city council and very concerned about his public image.'

Lavinia scoured the rest of the breakfast room, seeking out her next subject. Taggart took advantage of the brief pause to make a break for freedom. Bolting down the rest of his unappetising breakfast, he rose to his feet, smiling at Lavinia apologetically. 'You're quite right about the stewed fruit,' he told her. 'Keeps you regular as clockwork right enough.' With this excuse, he made a hasty exit, brushing past Ian Gowrie who was just coming in for his own breakfast.

Gowrie turned, staring after the departing Taggart with a thoughtful look on his face.

'Just like the rest of us,' came Gilbert Vance's voice in his ear. Gowrie whirled round. 'You're wondering what he's doing here, aren't you?' Vance went on. 'So we all are.'

Gowrie looked apologetic, feeling responsible for Taggart's presence. 'I didn't know who he was when I took the booking.'

Vance dismissed the apology with a shrug. 'You couldn't have been expected to. Nor, I suspect, were you intended to. Our Mr Taggart is a devious little man.'

'So what can he be after?' Gowrie wanted to know. 'He can't be looking for more evidence – there wouldn't be any point. They can't try Dr Napier a second time, not after a Not Proven verdict. It would be double jeopardy.'

Vance glanced at him with a somewhat surprised expression. 'Quite the amateur lawyer, aren't we?' he observed. 'You seem to have a few surprises up your sleeve, Ian.'

Gowrie smiled sheepishly. 'My father was a lawyer. Well, my adoptive father. It was what I wanted to be, once. It was all the reading which put me off.' He dropped the subject abruptly, as though it embarrassed him in some way. 'So what's your theory on why

Taggart's here?' he asked, rapidly changing the subject back again.

Vance was silent for a while, looking thoughtful and serious. 'Maybe he's not after Dr Napier at all,' he muttered, finally. He eyed Gowrie with a curious expression on his face. 'Maybe he's after someone else entirely.'

Chapter Seven

There was definitely something going on, Jardine had decided. All afternoon he had observed various colleagues sidling up to Jackie Reid in a most secretive manner, conduct short whispered conversations and then slink off again looking slightly guilty about something. It wasn't until he caught a quick glimpse of a five-pound note being slipped furtively into her palm that he finally figured it out.

Jardine wandered over to her desk, a disapproving look on his face. 'Strictly illegal, of course, running a book – but of course you know that,' he muttered.

Jackie looked up at him, her face clouding over. 'Aw, Mike, it's just a bit of fun,' she protested.

Jardine retained his stern expression for a few more

seconds until he could hold it no longer. Breaking into a grin, he let her off the hook. 'So, what are the current odds?' he asked.

Jackie smiled with relief. 'Six to four against Taggart lasting out,' she told him. 'Minimum bet a fiver.'

Jardine considered for a few moments, finally dipping into his back pocket. 'Okay – put me down for a tenner,' he murmured. '*For* him staying the course. That ought to be worth three to one at least.'

Jackie slipped the money into her desk and scribbled the entry into a spare notebook she had put aside for that express purpose. 'Such confidence,' she observed. 'You obviously have greater faith in the old man's will-power than the rest of us.'

Jardine smiled. 'Let's just say that I know what a dogged old goat he can be when he wants to. I take it that you don't think he'll make it?'

Jackie grinned knowingly. 'I'm absolutely sure he won't,' she said with total confidence. 'And what's more, I'm going to prove it. Want to come along for the ride?'

Jardine was intrigued. 'Where are we going?'

Jackie grinned. 'To see Taggart.' She fished under her desk and pulled out a bulging carrier-bag.

'What's in there?' Jardine wanted to know.

Jackie looked secretive. 'The bookie's equivalent of nobbling a horse,' she said mysteriously, and would give no further information.

Taggart was just preparing to go out, and had already put his coat on. Hearing the knock on his door, he hastily stripped it off again and threw it into the wardrobe. Slipping off his shoes, he kicked them under the bed and padded across the room towards the door in his socks.

He looked a little startled to see Jardine and Jackie Reid. He eyed them both suspiciously. 'What are you two doing here again?' he asked, rather ungraciously.

Jackie swept into the room without being invited. She had a good look around, then crossed to the bed and bounced up and down on it a couple of times. 'Very nice,' she said eventually, reaching a verdict. She looked up at Taggart. 'We come bearing gifts,' she announced cheerily.

'Oh, aye?' Taggart gave a very passable imitation of the guard on the gates of Troy.

Ignoring him, Jackie began to empty out the contents of her mysterious carrier-bag on to the bed, identifying each item as she produced it. 'Now I've got two Scotch pies, a packet of gingernut biscuits, four chocolate bars, a packet of individual apple turnovers and some crackers and cheese portions,' she announced. Delving back into the bag, she produced the *pièce de resistance*. 'Oh, and a bottle of Glenfiddich, of course. To wash things down with.'

Taggart regarded the foodstuffs warily. 'Where did all this stuff come from?' he wanted to know.

Jackie smiled at him. 'We had a whip-round in the office, sir. None of us wanted to see you starve.'

'Oh, I appreciate that,' Taggart muttered, obviously quite touched. 'But I'd also appreciate it if you'd pack all that stuff back into that bag and take it away with you.'

Jackie could only gape at him in total astonishment. Jardine had to turn away to conceal his smile.

'This place is a health farm,' Taggart went on. 'I'm here for my body and soul and I only have one of each. I have to stick very tightly to my individual diet programme.'

Jackie couldn't quite believe her ears. This was a Taggart she hardly recognised. She glanced at Jardine in a bemused fashion, as though he might be able to offer her some sort of explanation, but he merely grinned at her.

'Three to one, we said?' he murmured, in a very quiet voice. He turned his attention back to Taggart. 'Well, I suppose we'd better be going then, sir. No doubt you'll be wanting to turn in for a nice early night.' On afterthought, he paused. 'There's not much point in us inviting you to join us for a little night-cap then, I suppose? I noticed a rather nice-looking little pub just down the lane from here as we drove past.'

Taggart regarded him with an almost saintly expression. 'You go ahead and poison your systems if you want to,' he invited. 'Have a nice time.'

Jardine turned away and led the way out of the room, still grinning to himself. He was still looking totally smug – much to Jackie's annoyance – as they parked outside the pub and climbed out of the car.

'I don't know what's worse,' Jackie complained. 'The old Taggart or a newly converted one. That must be the biggest turn-around since Saul of Tarsus.'

Jardine shrugged philosophically. 'Mind you, you've got to hand it to him. He really seems to mean it. I reckon we could all be in for a few surprises when he comes back to work again.'

Jackie glowered at him, not relishing the prospect at all. 'I don't think I could stand the shock,' she muttered.

They walked into the pub. It was as welcoming and pleasant as it had appeared from the outside. A real olde worlde atmosphere, with a long wooden bar, genuine oak beams and a huge inglenook fireplace in which sweet-smelling logs crackled and burned cheerily.

The manager, John Roberts, looked every bit as traditional as his surroundings. Clad in a white dress-shirt and kilt, he was as immaculate as the bar was spotless. A perfect host, he greeted Jardine and Jackie warmly as they strolled in. 'Good evening to you,' he said, smiling. 'And what can I get for you?'

Jardine and Jackie perched themselves up on a pair of bar stools. 'Half a pint of bitter for me and a gin and tonic for the lady,' Jardine said. He paused, changing his mind with a grin. 'Actually, you'd better make that a double. She's just had a bit of a shock.'

'You're being uncommonly generous,' Jackie pointed out sarcastically, as the manager turned away to pour the drinks.

Jardine grinned at her. 'Oh, I think I can probably afford it – it'll come out of my winnings.'

Jackie gave him a baleful glare. 'You're really going to rub this one in, aren't you? Well, you haven't won yet.'

It was time to drop the matter, Jardine thought. Jackie Reid could only take so much ribbing before she got shirty. There was no point ruining a pleasant evening and atmosphere. He changed the subject, giving her a chance to relax again. 'Nice place,' he observed, glancing round the interior of the pub.

Surprisingly, there was only one other customer. A blonde-haired, heavily made-up woman in dark glasses who sat alone at the furthest table from the bar. She was smoking a long, thin black cigarette from an elegant silver holder and drinking a gin and bitter lemon. She looked like a Mata Hari impersonator, Jardine thought fancifully. Embarrassed in case he should be caught staring at her, he turned his eyes away and back to the bar. 'You're not too busy tonight,' Jardine observed conversationally as John Roberts placed the drinks down on the counter in front of them.

The man smiled easily. 'Oh, we never really get packed in here,' he said. 'Quiet, but steady, if you know what I mean. We're a little off the beaten track, you see.'

'And I suppose there having been a murder just down the road doesn't help trade much,' Jackie put in.

John ignored her. He held out his hand to Jardine. 'That will be three pounds twenty, sir,' he said politely but coldly. Taking the correct change that Jardine proffered, he moved away to the till, cashed it in and did not return.

Jardine and Jackie sipped at their drinks for a while, with nothing but the crackling and spitting of the log fire to break the silence. Finally, Jardine finished off his half-pint and glanced aside at Jackie. 'One more for the road?' he asked, somewhat half-heartedly.

Jackie shook her head. She knew he was only offering out of politeness, and she wasn't really in the mood anyway. She finished her own drink. 'No, let's go,' she muttered, sliding off her stool.

John watched them prepare to leave with a formal,

polite smile on his face. 'Goodnight,' he called out as they headed for the door. He busied himself polishing the already shining bar counter as they walked out. Mrs Drake looked up briefly with a slightly curious expression on her face and then returned her attention to her drink.

Jardine led the way to the car and let Jackie in to the passenger seat. Starting the engine, he backed in to the pub's small carpark to turn round then headed back up the lane towards the main road. The car's rear lights had hardly disappeared out of sight round the first bend before there was a rustling in the nearby bushes. A shadowy, furtive figure crept out, glancing anxiously around to make sure that no one had spotted him. Finally certain that he was unobserved, he scurried into the pub.

John flashed on his standard welcoming smile as Taggart slunk in, his coat pulled tight around his body. The smile quickly became a knowing grin as he recognised the now familiar shifty attitude and the tell-tale blue tracksuit bottoms showing beneath the bottom of Taggart's coat. 'Good evening, sir. I expect you'll want something warming after your walk in the night air.'

Taggart looked at him curiously. He was about to ask a question, then thought better of it. 'Aye, it's a little raw out there tonight,' he agreed. He glanced over to the blazing log fire and smiled. 'It's pretty cosy in here, though.'

'Always a warm welcome here, sir,' John assured him. 'So, what will it be for you, then?'

'I'll have a large dram, please,' Taggart told him.

John fished under the counter and produced a large

collection box, slapping it meaningfully on the bar top. 'That'll be fifty pence in the box then, sir.'

Taggart stared at the inscription written on the box: 'Escapee Penalty Fund'. He glanced at John questioningly for further explanation.

John looked a little smug. 'Tracksuit bottoms,' he said. 'Always a dead give-away. But a small price to pay, I consider. I don't tell them up at the health farm, and the local pensioners always get a good treat at Christmas.'

It was indeed a small price to pay, Taggart considered. He fished in his coat pocket and drew out a 50p piece, dropping it into the box. 'So what's the chances of a nice pie and chips as well?' he asked hopefully.

'No problem,' John assured him. 'But that'll be another pound in the box. Two, if you'll be wanting a sweet as well. If you don't mind taking a tip from me, sir – you're better off buying whisky by the double.'

Taggart's magnanimity was already stretched to breaking point, but he paid up anyway.

There was a self-satisfied smirk on John's face as he dropped the extra coins into the box. 'Thank you, sir. I'm a firm believer in making escapees pay, you see.'

'Very civic-minded of you,' Taggart grunted, with heavy sarcasm. He sat down to enjoy his very expensive whisky.

Behind him, Mrs Drake finished her drink, rose to her feet and began to walk towards the door. 'Goodnight, John,' she said as she passed Taggart's back.

Taggart turned on his bar stool, recognising the woman from the breakfast room. His eyes drifted down to her legs at the same time she regarded his. Identifying another identical blue tracksuit. Taggart smiled broadly.

'Oh, I almost forgot, sir,' John said suddenly. 'That'll be another two pound ten for the whisky.'

The smile faded from Taggart's face. Resignedly, he dipped into his pocket again. It was going to be a very expensive night.

Chapter Eight

The three months she had spent in prison waiting for her trial had taken their toll of her physical as well as her mental health, Janet Napier realised. She had become badly out of condition, and was now already fighting for breath after a jog of only two miles or so. Before the trial she would quite happily have completed a four-mile course and still have had enough stamina in reserve to do half an hour's workout in the health resort's gym when she got back.

It was the first morning she had managed to get back to her regular exercise régime, and it had turned out an absolute disaster. Utterly exhausted, and with a painful stitch in her side, Janet finally gave up and ground to a halt opposite the pub which she would normally have sprinted past. She leaned back against a tree for support, panting heavily. She cast her eyes about, looking for somewhere a bit more comfortable to sit and rest. It was with mixed feelings that she recognised the car which was parked directly outside the entrance to the pub. It was Jeremy's.

Her initial sense of relief was quickly dampened by the earliness of the hour. Janet glanced at her watch, noting that it was only a couple of minutes past eleven o'clock. Her son must have been virtually waiting outside the door at opening time. It was just another sign to join the others which she had noted over the last few days: the smell of drink which seemed to pervade his room, the bleary eyes and hangovers at the breakfast table, his general jumpiness and the speed with which his mood could now turn to anger.

She was a doctor as well as a mother, but it didn't take a wealth of medical knowledge to recognise that her son was beginning to exhibit many of the symptoms of someone with a drink problem. She could only hope that it was a temporary thing, his own reaction to the stress which had torn the family apart over the months.

Painfully, Janet dragged herself across the road to the pub, peering inside as she passed the window. Jeremy was perched up at the bar with a glass in front of him, deep in conversation with John, the manager. Janet moved along to the door and staggered in, collapsing on the nearest chair.

Jeremy looked surprised, and more than a little guilty, to see her. He was immediately on the defensive, even before she had said a word. He held up the glass of

carefully laid slices of freshly cut cucumber over her face and neck. 'There, Mrs Jeffrey, that will cleanse your pores. How does it feel?'

'Fine, thank you – although I do feel a bit like a tossed salad,' Lavinia joked. She broke off as the door opened with a sigh and Belinda turned towards it. Taking advantage of the situation, Lavinia's hand snaked out to pick two or three cucumber slices off her face and stuff them into her mouth, quickly chewing them up and swallowing greedily.

Belinda frowned as her mother walked straight in, ignoring Lavinia's presence. 'Look, you can see I'm busy,' she protested, resenting the sudden intrusion.

'We need to have that talk,' Janet said, quietly but firmly. 'How about this evening?'

Belinda shook her head. 'Not tonight. I'm going out to see a show. There's a troupe of African dancers appearing in cabaret at the Tropicana Club in Glasgow.'

Janet's face darkened, feeling a rising tide of impotent anger building up inside her. She felt like screaming at her daughter, taking hold of her and shaking her like a ragdoll, but was not prepared for a scene in front of one of the guests. Instead, she contained her frustration as best she could, merely nodding curtly. 'What about tonight? What time will you be home?'

'Late,' Belinda said brusquely. 'Very late, I expect.'

There was nothing else to be said. Dejectedly, Janet turned and walked out again, slamming the door behind her.

Her angry departure left a vacuum of silent tension in the room, which Lavinia Jeffrey was quick to fill.

'African dancers, eh?' she observed. 'Sounds rather erotic.'

Belinda shook her head. 'No, not really. I don't even think it's my cup of tea.'

Under the layers of cucumber, Lavinia smiled knowingly. 'Ah, just going to please the boyfriend then, are we?' she wanted to know, hungry for the slightest tit-bit of gossip.

'Hardly,' Belinda answered her. 'I'm going with my father. He likes that sort of thing. Says it reminds him of home.'

Chapter Nine

In fact, Belinda enjoyed the show much more than she had expected to. It was colourful, fast-paced and crackled with a raw, earthy vibrance which she found strangely exciting, and the heady rhythms of the African music seemed to strike a chord in her memory which spoke of happier times. Even though she had actually been born some years after her parents had left South Africa, it was somehow locked into her genes, and it was as if she carried a small part of it in her blood.

Strangely, the evening seemed to have a negative effect on her father. Far from cheering up Gerald Napier, the show appeared to depress him. Throughout the evening he became progressively more ill at ease, even irritable. He drank far more than he usually did, and was clearly in no fit state to drive home when the spectacular cabaret finally ended with an impressive display of simulated battle and spear-throwing.

By the time Belinda had driven him safely home to the Glasgow flat and shared a nightcap, it was already well after one in the morning. But despite the lateness of the hour, she was in no particular hurry as she began the long drive back to the health farm. The later she arrived home, the less likely it was that her mother would be waiting up for her, and she had a busy working schedule for the following day. With luck, their threatened clash could be postponed for at least another twenty-four hours.

With this comforting thought in mind, Belinda slipped a Chris Rea tape into the car's stereo system and relaxed. She drove carefully, aware that although she was by no means drunk, she had consumed enough glasses of wine to slow down her reactions. Just under an hour later, she turned off the main road on to the lane which led home, dropping her speed. Cruising along at just over twenty-five miles an hour, she was feeling mellow and perfectly at ease as the BMW's superb suspension creamed out the ruts and bumps in the country lane.

Ahead of her, just before the sign which announced the turn-off to the Napier Health Resort, the car's headlights suddenly picked up something in the middle of the road. Thinking that it might be a dead or wounded animal, Belinda slowed right down, dropping to a mere crawl as she strained her eyes through the windscreen, trying to make out what it was.

She brought the car to a complete halt as she finally

identified the weird obstacle. It was a small wooden chair, the sort of thing which might be found in a child's nursery or playroom. And, seated in the chair, its glassy eyes reflecting the beam of the car headlights, was seated a black, life-sized baby doll.

Belinda stared at it dumbly for some time, racking her brains for an explanation. It didn't make sense. The chair was positioned too perfectly in the exact middle of the lane for it to have fallen there accidentally. Which meant that it had been set up with careful deliberation – but why? Belinda asked herself. Perhaps it was a child's game, she thought for a moment, then realised that no children lived in the immediate vicinity. There was only the Sampson farm, the pub, a couple of retired farm workers' cottages, and the health resort.

So it had to be a prank of some sort, Belinda reasoned – although she could figure out no reason nor any possible perpetrator. If it was a joke, it appeared to be a rather pointless one – and if anything, it was more sinister than funny. Illuminated in the glare of the headlights, the black doll seemed almost evil, like some sort of a voodoo symbol.

The first faint stirrings of unease began to creep into her body like a chill, negating the comfortable warmth of the car's interior. Belinda shivered slightly, toying with the idea of just slamming the BMW into gear and driving right over the thing. But the chair looked chunky and substantial, and quite capable of doing the expensive car more than superficial damage. There was no room to drive around it. It would have to be moved, Belinda realised, uncomfortably.

She was beginning to feel really frightened now.

Cautiously, she opened the car door and stepped out, gazing fearfully around the gloomy shadows in the penumbra of the car lights. There was no sound, other than the faint murmur of the breeze through the tops of the trees, and no sign of life except a faint yellow light from the Sampson farmhouse buildings a quarter of a mile away. Leaving the car door open, Belinda took a deep breath and ran to the doll in the chair, lifting them both together and flinging them to the side of the road.

She began to turn back towards the car. Suddenly, she was in total blackness as the headlights snapped off. For just a split second, Belinda caught a glimpse of a shadowy figure standing by the open door, and then it had melted into the greater blackness of the night.

A numbing sense of terror ripped through her, threatening to freeze her in her tracks. She opened her mouth to scream, but nothing came out except a strangled sob. A jolt of adrenaline coursed through her system, triggering the 'fight or flight' response. Exploding into sudden action, Belinda began to run with the desperation of a trapped animal. She was only vaguely aware that she was running in the direction of the Sampson farmhouse, some instinct for survival deep in her subconscious making her head for the light, the last symbol of safety she had seen.

Thick mud sucked at her high-heeled shoes, making every step a struggle. Belinda kicked them off, knowing that she could run faster in her stockinged feet. Brambles and gorse bushes tore at her legs, but she was oblivious to the pain as she stumbled through the undergrowth towards the open fields surrounding the farmhouse.

She ran into a wire fence, which threatened to cage

her. Whimpering with fear, Belinda struggled over it, shredding her clothing on the single strand of barbed wire which ran along the top. Nothing mattered now except reaching the safety of the light. Clearing the fence, she began to run again. Behind her, she heard the thud of footsteps and a sudden grunt of pain as her pursuer also encountered the fence.

Several times Belinda stumbled and fell, but sheer terror picked her up each time and set her aching legs moving again. She was exhausted now, her lungs bursting. She was no longer really running, merely fleeing by whatever means she could manage. Staggering, shambling, sometimes half-crawling, she struggled towards the light as the sounds of pursuit grew louder and nearer.

It was a cow byre, the source of light only a single electric lamp over the door to deter foxes from preying upon the free-range chickens who used the building as a night roost. There was no salvation here, Belinda realised with a sinking heart. No one to save her, even to help her. But perhaps the building itself could offer sanctuary. Frantically, Belinda crashed against the door, which sagged open on old and rusted hinges. She staggered inside, ploughing through a thick layer of matted, stinking straw which covered the floor of the barn.

She stopped abruptly, pivoting to throw her weight back against the door in a desperate attempt to close and seal it against the terrors which pursued her.

And, in that terrible second, she saw the face of her pursuer, thrown into sharp relief under the light. Belinda's eyes opened wide with fear and incomprehension, then dropped to the glinting, ugly weapon which was to be the instrument of her death.

She was no longer in any doubt that she was about to die. Yet the instinct for survival was still strong. Belinda turned again, preparing to flee once more even though there was no place left to run.

She managed just three steps before the wicked blade plunged into her back. With a single, guttural grunt, she fell forwards into the straw and lay motionless. Blood seeped from her mouth into the stinking straw, mingling with the other dark stains of mud and cow dung.

The cows, with the bovine passivity and stupidity of their species, merely looked down at her body with mute disinterest, swishing their tails slowly from side to side as they stepped around it.

It was a cold, grey morning. Jardine and Jackie Reid were already outside the cow byre when McVitie arrived. He walked across to them from the police car, his craggy face wrinkled in disgust as he picked his way through a mire of mud and cow dung. 'Who found her?' he demanded.

'The farmer, Bill Sampson,' Jardine told him. 'He knows her by sight, so he was able to identify her immediately. He called the local bobby right away, who came straight through to us.'

McVitie digested the information and nodded. 'Has Dr Andrews got here yet?' he asked.

Jardine jerked his thumb towards the interior of the byre. 'He's examining the body now, sir.' Jardine paused.

'Do you want me to inform Chief Inspector Taggart, sir?'

McVitie's face darkened. 'You most certainly will *not* inform Chief Inspector Taggart,' he thundered emphatically. 'I'll be taking charge of this case personally.'

Jardine flashed a dubious glance at Jackie Reid as McVitie stormed past him. 'That'll upset the old man when he *does* find out,' he muttered, under his breath.

Jackie could picture Taggart's outraged face in her mind. It was not a pretty sight. Her own expression registered the extent of Jardine's understatement. 'Upset him? He'll have a seizure.'

Dr Andrews was still bending over Belinda's body as McVitie approached him. 'Well, what can you tell me so far?'

Andrews straightened up, regarding McVitie with a grim face. 'This may not be about to make your day,' he started warily, 'But death was caused by a single knife wound which seems to be extremely deep. In the back, between the second and third lower vertebrae.'

'Any sign of the murder weapon?' McVitie wanted to know.

Andrews shook his head. 'Nothing has shown up so far. I assume you'll order a thorough sweep search of the surrounding area.'

McVitie grunted. He was extremely touchy about any suggestion of someone apparently telling him how to do his job. 'Well, can you at least give me some indication of what sort of weapon we'll be looking for?' he asked.

'Not until I've conducted a full autopsy back in the lab,' Andrews told him. 'But if you want an instant, on-the-spot opinion, I'd say this wound is totally consistent with that on another victim I examined not half a mile from here three months ago. In fact, I'd go so far as to say identical.'

'You're suggesting that this was the same weapon that was used in the Caroline Kemp killing?' McVitie queried.

'And most probably the same murderer,' Andrews confirmed. 'A single, powerful thrust in exactly the right place to cause virtually instantaneous death. This killer knows exactly what he, or she, is doing.'

McVitie was silent for a moment. Andrews was right. The information most definitely did *not* make his day. It was every police officer's private nightmare to come up against a serial killer on the rampage. He tried to push the unpalatable thought out of his mind for the time being. 'You said "powerful", Doctor,' he went on. 'How much force would be required to deliver a killing blow like that?'

'A great deal of force,' Andrews said emphatically. He paused thoughtfully. 'If you remember, I made that point at Dr Napier's trial – but I'm making it again now.'

Jardine and Jackie Reid had come in to join them. Jardine knelt down by the body. He lifted one of Belinda's legs and examined it. 'Look at the state of her feet, sir,' he pointed out to McVitie. 'She obviously ran across open country all the way from her car.'

'We found that abandoned back in the lane,' Jackie Reid put in. 'Apparently untouched, keys still in the ignition. No sign of any struggle there, or any indication that she might have had anyone with her. The passenger door was locked from the inside.'

'So someone was waiting for her,' McVitie mused. 'But why would she stop on a deserted country lane in the middle of the night – unless it was for someone she knew? A lover's tryst, perhaps? One that went wrong?' He looked across at Andrews again as a sudden thought struck him. 'Any indications of sexual assault?' he asked, almost hopefully.

He was to be disappointed. Andrews shook his head. 'None whatsoever,' he said with total confidence. 'Whoever did this had cold-blooded murder on their mind, and nothing else.' He paused briefly, shaking his head slowly from side to side. 'That's the other thing which I find very strange about this case.'

'Strange?' Jardine picked up on the word at once.

Andrews nodded. 'Yes, it doesn't seem to fit with the normal patterns of knife attacks. There's no sign of any other injury. In my experience, people who kill with knives do not stop at a single blow. Invariably, it is a frenzied, repeated attack which leaves multiple wounds. Both in this case and in the case of Caroline Kemp, there is something curiously *precise* – I might even say restrained – about the killings.'

'Perhaps we're dealing with a squeamish murderer who doesn't like the sight of blood,' Jackie suggested sarcastically.

It was not appreciated. This was made painfully obvious by the glaring looks which Andrews, McVitie and Jardine all threw in her direction.

Andrews was thoughtfully silent for some time, finally glancing uncertainly from McVitie to Jardine in turn as though he wasn't sure whether to voice his thoughts or not.

'Do you have some sort of a theory?' McVitie asked, clutching at straws.

Andrews looked guarded. 'Not what you might call a theory as such – more of an observation,' he muttered. 'But if you were to ask me for an instinctive reaction to these killings – I'd say that they bear all the hallmarks of an execution, rather than a murder.'

It was a pretty fine distinction, Jardine thought. But, nevertheless, something to think about.

Chapter Ten

The breakfasts didn't seem to get any better, Taggart reflected morosely, staring at the bowl of stewed prunes which Gilbert Vance had just thrust under his nose. Unable to face them without building up to it, he sipped at his glass of fruit juice and nibbled on the single slice of unbuttered toast which his spartan diet allowed him.

Lavinia Jeffrey swept into the breakfast room, looking disgustingly bright and breezy. She headed straight for Taggart's table, much to his annoyance. The woman seemed to have adopted him as a sort of fellow spirit, for some unaccountable reason. 'Well, it's certainly all happening this morning,' she announced brightly, sitting down opposite him.

It was a baited statement, begging his curiosity. Taggart regarded her with mild interest. Her face was flushed with excitement and the sheer joy of having a big secret all to herself. The look in her eyes told him that she was almost bursting to share it.

Even conversation with Lavinia might be slightly preferable to cold stewed prunes, Taggart thought. 'Why, what's going on?' he asked.

Lavinia's eyes flashed conspiratorially. 'Whatever it is, it's something pretty big,' she whispered. 'There are police officers crawling all over reception out there. Do you suppose it's some sort of raid? What is it they call it . . . a bust? Could it be drugs, do you suppose . . . something like that?'

Taggart didn't wait for any further speculation. Somehow the fanciful idea of cannabis in the carrot juice didn't quite gel. However, any sort of police activity was definitely something which demanded his attention. He was on his feet in a flash, mumbling a hasty apology to Lavinia as he hurried out of the breakfast room.

There was definitely something going on, although 'crawling with policemen' was probably something of an overstatement. Taggart's eyes took in the scene around him with practised efficiency. Superintendent McVitie was talking to Ian Gowrie while Jardine and Jackie Reid merely stood on either side of the front door like a pair of sentinels. Edging warily past his superior's back, Taggart grabbed Jackie by the arm and pulled her aside. 'What's going on?' he hissed in her ear.

Before she could answer him, a heavy hand

descended on Taggart's shoulder. 'I'll handle this, DC Reid,' came McVitie's gruff voice. Forcefully, he propelled Taggart across the reception area to the empty guest room. Pushing him inside, he closed the double doors for privacy and stood with his back to them, holding Taggart with a reproving stare. 'You are not to interfere in this one, Jim. Is that clearly understood?'

Taggart glared back at him indignantly. 'With respect, sir – I have a right to know what's going on.'

McVitie wrinkled his nose and sniffed. He continued staring at Taggart in silence for a few seconds. 'All right,' he conceded eventually. 'I suppose I can't stop you from knowing what's happened, because you're bound to find out sooner or later. But that's as far as it goes.' He paused for a moment, framing the bare facts in his head. 'It's Belinda Napier. She's been murdered. It happened last night.'

Taggart gaped at him, temporarily stunned with shock. Recovering himself, he moved to push past McVitie and open the doors.

'Where do you think you're going?' McVitie demanded.

Taggart looked at his superior in surprise. 'I'm going up to my room to change out of this tracksuit.'

McVitie's face darkened. He placed the flat of his hand squarely against Taggart's chest. 'You most certainly are *not* going to change out of your tracksuit!' he thundered.

Taggart's eyes took on a pleading look. 'Aw, sir – I can hardly take charge of an investigation dressed like this,' he complained.

McVitie sighed deeply. He was obviously not getting

his message across to the man. He tried again, this time a little more forcefully. 'You are not taking charge of this investigation. You are not taking any part in this investigation. What is more, you are not going to even *think* about this investigation. Do I make myself clear? I'm going to handle it personally. You came here to rest, and that's exactly what you're going to do – *rest*!'

Even this did not seem to put Taggart in his place. He faced up to McVitie squarely, almost aggressively, preparing to launch into another protest.

He never got the chance. McVitie's patience snapped. 'I can't order you to leave this place,' he spluttered angrily. 'But if I find you so much as even try to interfere, I will have you hauled over more hot coals than . . .' He broke off awkwardly, his anger rendering him speechless for a moment.

'A roast chestnut?' Taggart suggested helpfully.

McVitie shot him a withering glare. 'Yes, something like that,' he agreed weakly. He half-turned to open the doors at last.

Taggart was crushed, but not yet quite beaten. He had one last little card up his sleeve. 'The night Caroline Kemp was murdered, it seems she had borrowed Belinda's car,' he announced. 'The two girls were similar in appearance, and might easily have been confused for each other in the dark.' He stared McVitie in the face, raising one eyebrow querulously. 'Now doesn't that make you wonder whether Belinda might have been the intended victim all along?'

McVitie merely glared at him, with a look which suggested that he was perfectly capable of working that one out for himself. Then, without another word, he opened the doors and stomped out of the guest room, leaving Taggart standing there like a child who had just had his lollipop stolen.

Janet Napier looked a broken woman. All the calm pride, almost bravado, which she had affected throughout the trial appeared to have deserted her. She sat stiffly against the back of the chesterfield, as though paralysed with shock. Jeremy sat beside her, his arm wrapped tightly around her shoulder, hugging her.

Janet's eyes rolled distractedly in their sockets. Her lips moved weakly. 'My God – what's happening to us?' she whispered, unable to accept, let alone deal with, this new trauma.

Jeremy glared up at McVitie, Jardine and Jackie Reid with a look of open hostility. 'Do you have to speak to her now?' he demanded angrily. 'Can't you see what a state of shock she's in?'

McVitie nodded slowly. His tone was apologetic, but insistent. 'Yes, I'm afraid we do,' he murmured.

'Can either of you think of any reason why someone might have wanted to kill Belinda?' Jardine put in.

Jeremy turned on him with a scathing anger blazing in his eyes. 'Why do the police always ask such bloody stupid questions?' he demanded.

Janet Napier seemed to regain control of herself, Jackie Reid noticed. There was a strange, worried look in her eyes which was almost fear. It was as if she was afraid of the true extent of her son's anger and was moved to protect him. It was a curious situation, Jackie reflected. The over-protective son and the protective mother. But who was protecting whom?

Janet moved her hand gently to her son's knee, patting it reassuringly. 'Please, Jeremy,' she entreated him. 'It's all right.'

But Jeremy was not going to be pacified. His anger, always on a hair-trigger, had been fired now. He jumped to his feet, his voice rising to a shout. 'No, it's not all right! It's not all right at all!' He faced up to Jardine again in an aggressive posture. 'You lot have put my mother through hell,' he blazed. 'And now you come round here with your stupid notebooks and your damned platitudes and you want to know who killed my sister? Well, you lot did. You killed our entire family, that's what you did!'

His rage seemed to subside as fast as it had risen. He sank back into the chesterfield, cuddling his mother and staring up at Jardine in sullen anger.

Jardine flashed a questioning glance at McVitie, who merely shrugged. He didn't seem to know quite what to do. It was a stalemate situation, in which everyone felt equally awkward. Finally, there seemed no option but to back off. 'We'll probably have to speak to you again,' McVitie told Jeremy and Janet a trifle lamely. He turned to Jardine. 'I want statements from every employee, every current guest and every regular or past guest over the last two years.' He began to walk towards the door.

'Does that list include Chief Inspector Taggart, sir?' Jackie wanted to know as they reached the corridor.

McVitie gave her a pained look, as if the mere mention of the man's name was now enough to cause him anguish. 'Yes, that includes Chief Inspector Taggart.'

They walked along the landing towards the staircase. 'What about Belinda's old boyfriends, sir?' Jardine asked when they were well away from the Napiers' living-room. 'I suppose you'll be wanting to speak to them as well. Jealousy can be a powerful motive for murder.'

McVitie nodded. 'I'll leave that to you two,' he muttered. 'Right now I'm going to speak to the father.'

'I don't envy you that job, sir,' Jackie observed. 'I understand he and Belinda were very close.'

McVitie frowned, allowing himself to think about it. He was getting too many reminders that he had been stuck behind a desk for too long. He had almost forgot-ten some of the less pleasant aspects of the job. The task would be better left to Taggart, he found himself thinking ruefully. He had a daughter – and he had his feet and his heart firmly out on the streets. He would probably make a better job of it. Just for a moment, McVitie found him-self regretting his impetuous decision to exclude Taggart from the case, but he wasn't going to let Jardine or Jackie Reid see it. What was done was done, and he had to make the best of it.

'Just make sure that nobody leaves this place with-out being interviewed,' he snapped at them. Reaching the top of the stairs, he quickened his pace and began to stride down them in a purposeful fashion, making it perfectly clear that he was leaving them in charge.

'Well, I suppose we might as well get the worst part over first,' Jackie Reid suggested as McVitie's back disap-peared out through the front door.

Jardine studied the thin smile on her face, not quite following her chain of thought. 'What's the worst part?' he wanted to know.

Jackie grinned at him. 'Getting a statement from Taggart,' she said. 'Do you want to do the honours, or shall I?'

Jardine set his face in grim determination. 'We'll both do it,' he announced firmly. 'But first we have to find him.'

The man in question was at that moment wallowing in a bath of thick black mud, and not enjoying it very much at all. Feeling extremely stupid and embarrassed, he sat stiffly upright in the tub, despite Nurse Clark's constant exhortations for him to relax.

'Come along, Mr Taggart. You're supposed to sink back right into it, let the hot mud soak into all those poison-filled pores of yours.' She prodded his stiff shoulders, trying to physically push him under the surface.

Taggart resisted heartily, holding tight on to the sides of the bath. 'You might have poison in *your* pores,' he told her indignantly, 'but I'm quite happy with mine the way they are.'

Nurse Clark tried another approach, working on the popular hypothesis that all men are merely little boys at heart. 'Are you telling me that a tough policeman like you is afraid of a little mud?' she taunted him. The change of tactic worked. It was a direct challenge which Taggart was unable to resist. Relinquishing his grip on the sides of the tub, he allowed his body to sink down until the mud came up to the level of his chin. Nurse Clark smiled triumphantly. 'There now – isn't that better?'

Taggart merely glowered at her. 'It might be if I was

a hippo,' he muttered unhappily.

There was a knock on the treatment-room door. Nurse Clark turned towards it, protective as a mother hen hatching out chicks. 'You can't come in here,' she called out.

Her instruction went unheeded. The door opened and Jardine and Jackie strode in, looking suitably apologetic. They both viewed Taggart in the mud bath with obvious amusement.

Taggart regarded them balefully. Caught like this, he was feeling extremely vulnerable. 'What do you two want?' he growled aggressively. He threw another withering glance in Nurse Clark's direction, willing her to make herself scarce. Discretion being the better part of valour in this case, she found an excuse to tend to another client in an adjoining cubicle and slunk away.

'Well?' Taggart demanded gruffly, looking up at his two colleagues again. 'You'd better have a pretty good reason for this little visit.'

Jardine struggled to keep a straight face. The sight of his superior sitting naked in a bath of mud was something he could not have imagined in his wildest fantasies. Totally failing in her own self-control, Jackie Reid had to look away to hide the smirk on her face. 'Sorry, sir, but The Biscuit wants a statement,' Jardine explained, 'about the last time you saw or spoke to Belinda Napier. He was quite adamant that we spoke to you.'

'A statement?' Taggart echoed. He thought for a moment. 'Well, how about this. You just follow the theory that Belinda Napier was the intended victim from the beginning. That the killer only murdered Caroline Kemp by mistake.'

Jardine was surprised, but he took the time to think it through. As a theory it was fair enough, but it did raise a few other issues – one of which Taggart might not find very palatable. 'But that would mean that we were wrong about Janet Napier all along,' he pointed out.

The thought had also occurred to Taggart, and he found it slightly embarrassing. He was not a man to admit his mistakes too readily. Devoid of a suitable answer, he lay back in the mud, saying nothing.

'Why would the murderer wait so long, sir?' Jackie wanted to know, getting back into the conversation. 'It's been over three months.'

A vague and sluggish movement underneath the mud suggested that Taggart had shrugged his shoulders. 'I'm not on this case,' he muttered bitterly. 'You'll have to work that one out for yourselves.'

Jardine fidgeted awkwardly. 'I still have to take that statement, sir,' he pointed out. 'The Biscuit was very insistent.'

Taggart raised himself into a sitting position again and extended a muddy arm in Jardine's direction. 'Here – give me your notebook,' he snapped. 'I'll give him a statement.'

Dubiously, Jardine held out his pristine notebook and a pen. Taggart snatched them both, scribbled quickly and handed it back.

Jardine accepted the mud-splattered pad gingerly, reading the single expletive which Taggart had written. He regarded his superior with renewed respect, almost bordering on hero-worship. 'You really want me to show this to Superintendent McVitie?' he asked in an awe-struck voice.

Taggart sank back into his mud-bath, grinning up at Jardine roguishly. 'Oh, aye – but don't expect me to sign it,' he muttered.

Chapter Eleven

'Oh, Mr Taggart,' Ian Gowrie called out from the reception desk as Taggart strolled past on his way to the dining-room for lunch.

Taggart sauntered over to the desk. 'What is it?'

'Your wife telephoned a few minutes ago, while you were in the treatment room,' Gowrie informed him.

Taggart blanched a little. He hadn't called Jean since his arrival at the health resort. It could have been a mistake. 'And what did you tell her?' he asked, warily.

Gowrie was politely efficient. 'Exactly what you instructed, Mr Taggart. That you were not accepting calls of any kind because you are trying to avoid stress.'

Taggart smiled with relief. So far it didn't sound too bad. 'Did she leave any message?' he wanted to know.

Gowrie kept a straight face. 'Only that she would show you what stress was when you got home. Or words to that effect, anyway.'

Taggart could imagine what the 'words to that effect' actually were. However, it was a problem he would face when he came to it. Still smiling to himself, he continued on his way into the dining-room. The smile faded abruptly as he walked through the double doors. Lavinia Jeffrey had already installed herself at his table. She was rapidly becoming a regular fixture of every meal, Taggart reflected gloomily. The food was bad enough without her constant prattle to further damage his digestion. She preened visibly as he approached, reminding him of a very fat spider sitting in her web and waiting for a fly.

'Had a nice morning?' she enquired as he sat down.

Taggart merely grunted and picked up the menu. Gilbert Vance scurried over, his order pad in his hand. He smiled down at Taggart in a patronising manner. 'Good news, Mr Taggart. You're allowed a choice today. You can have lentil and corn pie, a little light chicken salad, or the millet and vegetable fricassee. Or today's special, of course – which happens to be a personal favourite of mine: savoury carrot layer.'

If Taggart was supposed to be pleased, he didn't show it. He was still waiting for the good news he had been promised. 'I'll take the pie,' he muttered, without any great enthusiasm.

'That comes with mashed potato on top, not pie crust, you realise,' Vance pointed out.

Taggart shrugged philosophically. 'Just as long as there's more than one lentil underneath it.'

Lavinia laid her hand on his arm as Vance flounced away with a look of contempt on his face. 'Do I detect the first signs of cracking?' she enquired gently.

Taggart discreetly removed his arm, under the pretext of unfolding his table napkin. 'I just object to being treated like a budgie.' He tried to steer the conversation to potentially more productive lines. 'Have you had your interview with the police yet?'

Lavinia grasped his arm again, adopting her infuriating confidential and intimate manner. 'It was simply awful. I had to answer dozens of questions. But I think I was very useful to them.'

'Useful?' Taggart picked up on the word hopefully.

Lavinia nodded. 'You see, I might be one of the last people to have spoken to Belinda before she went out last night. She was going out to a nightclub with her father. Some African dancers, she told me.' She squeezed Taggart's arm. 'I find it quite scary, imagining that some homicidal maniac is walking around out there. I mean, a woman on her own just isn't safe anymore, is she?'

Taggart resisted the impulse to point out that she would probably be quite safe in a rugby club shower room. He was uncomfortably aware that Lavinia was now fondling his arm in a most familiar manner. Opening the conversation appeared to have been something of a mistake. From the corner of his eye, he caught a glimpse of Janet Napier walking through the kitchen door into the dining-room.

Time to kill two birds with one stone, Taggart thought. He rose to his feet, smiling politely down at Lavinia. 'Excuse me, but I need to speak to Dr Napier for a moment.'

He caught up with her just as she was walking out into the reception lobby. 'Dr Napier – could I have a word with you, please?'

Janet regarded him with tired, heavy eyes. 'Mr Taggart, I really don't believe I have anything to say to you. I've been answering questions from your colleagues all morning, and I've told them everything I can.'

Taggart gave her a sympathetic, friendly smile. 'There aren't any questions, Dr Napier. I have something I want to say to you.'

Janet studied his face carefully for a few seconds, finally sighing. 'All right,' she murmured in a weary voice. She walked a few yards across the lobby to a quiet corner and stopped, turning to confront him. 'Now, what is it, Mr Taggart?'

Having come this far, Taggart suddenly felt embarrassed and awkward. It wasn't in his nature to be humble. He was silent for a while, trying to choose his words carefully. 'Look, sometimes the police make mistakes,' he started, hesitantly. 'Or they get railroaded into making wrong assumptions. Like thinking someone is guilty when they aren't.'

Janet held his eyes in a cool stare. 'Isn't that why we have juries?' she asked quietly.

She wasn't going to make it easy, Taggart realised, and he couldn't really blame her. 'Sometimes even juries get it wrong,' he admitted.

Janet Napier was silent for a few seconds, apparently adjusting to this new Taggart. When she finally spoke again, there was a thin, almost wistful smile underlying the sadness on her face. 'Mr Taggart – if I'd been found guilty, a lot of people would have been convinced that I

116

was innocent. Or if I'd been acquitted, some might still have thought I was guilty, but I could have coped with that.' She paused, momentarily. 'That's why Not Proven is a sentence in itself, the worst possible verdict of all. It's an open-ended sentence, a never-ending one. Of people not knowing, of not knowing oneself whether those nearest to you believe in you or not. Do you understand what I mean?'

Taggart nodded slowly. 'I think I know what you're trying to say, Dr Napier – and I'm sorry.'

Janet could still not bring herself to acknowledge the apology. 'Will that be all, Mr Taggart?' she enquired.

There was nothing more he could say, Taggart realised. But before he let her go, the detective in him struggled to the surface. 'Can you think of any reason why anyone would have wanted to kill your daughter all those months ago – and then, knowing that they'd got it wrong, waited to try again?'

Janet's face hardened. 'No,' she said flatly.

'I'm sorry,' Taggart murmured, realising that he'd gone beyond his original intentions. 'I promised you no questions.'

Janet studied his face for a while, seeing the look of abject humility there and realising how hard it must be for the man. She relented, finally. 'Thank you for apologising, Mr Taggart.'

She turned and began to walk away. Despite her acceptance of his apology, Taggart felt a burning need to justify himself a little more. 'Doctor,' he called after her.

Janet turned, questioning him with her eyes. 'We all make mistakes. You must have made some in your own career,' Taggart pointed out.

Janet's mouth dropped open slightly. For a brief second, it looked as though she was going to answer him, but she remained silent. She stared at him for a long time with a strange, sad, faraway look in her eyes. Then she walked away, leaving Taggart standing there awkwardly.

McVitie was feeling equally ill at ease, having broken the tragic news of Belinda's murder to Gerald Napier. His earlier fears had been confirmed; he had been away from street police work for too long to retain the feel for personal contact. Murder had become little more than a piece of paperwork, another statistic. It wasn't that he couldn't understand Napier's grief – he just couldn't empathise with it.

Napier's initial shock and outrage had begun to dissipate slightly now, leaving him about to slide into a morass of self-pity. 'My Belle, my Belle,' he moaned softly, under his breath.

'Your belle?' McVitie prompted, gingerly.

Napier took a deep, sobbing breath, nodding his head faintly. 'I always called her that. It was a pet name . . . you know how you give them to kids. Belle of the Ball . . . she was always so beautiful, you see.' These last words came out of Napier's mouth on a rising sob. The man appeared to be on the verge of breaking down into tears, increasing McVitie's sense of discomfiture.

Rescue came unexpectedly. There was a gentle tap on the consulting-room door, and Agnes Pollock started to come in. Her intrusion served to drag Napier back from the brink. Pulling himself together with a conscious and visible effort, he sat stiffly upright at his desk and faced his receptionist with a composed expression. 'Yes, Agnes? What is it?'

The woman held a letter in her hand, immediately identifiable by the way the name and address on the envelope were scrawled in crude block capitals. 'Another one of those horrible letters arrived. I thought the detective would want to see it.'

'I'll take that,' McVitie said, reaching out to take the envelope from her hand. He paused before opening it, aware that Agnes was continuing to stand there, obviously wanting to be a part of things. He glanced at Napier, raising one eyebrow in a questioning gesture.

The man got the message. He nodded at his receptionist. 'Yes, thank you, Agnes. That will be all.'

McVitie could not miss the look of hurt and disappointment which crossed the receptionist's face. There was obviously something between them, he noted – although whether it was a one-way or a two-way thing, he had no way of telling. He waited until Agnes had reluctantly backed out of the consulting room and closed the door behind her before ripping open the envelope and carefully extracting the single sheet inside with the aid of a clean handkerchief.

The message was exactly the same as all the others. 'WHAT DOES IT FEEL LIKE TO BE MARRIED TO A MURDERESS?'

McVitie showed it to Napier briefly before slipping it back into the envelope and transferring it to his pocket. 'You're sure you have no idea who might be sending these letters?' he asked Napier.

The man shook his head. 'None whatsoever.'

'And you've made no enemies that you can think of? There's no one who might hold some sort of a grudge against you or your family?'

'No one I can think of.' Napier seemed pretty definite. He looked up at McVitie with a pleading look. 'Will that be all for now, Superintendent? I need to call my wife.'

'Of course.' McVitie felt awkward and out of place again. He turned to leave, when his eyes fell upon a framed qualification certificate on the wall. It was issued by the University of Durban. 'How long have you lived in this country, Dr Napier?' McVitie asked.

'Twenty years,' Napier answered him. 'Janet and I came back together.'

'Any particular reason for leaving South Africa?' McVitie wanted to know. It was idle curiosity more than anything else, but the question seemed to throw Napier slightly. The man's face clouded over, as though some unpleasant or uncomfortable memory had been stirred. He seemed suddenly a trifle evasive. 'No real reason,' he muttered. 'It was Janet who wanted to come back, that was all. We'd already decided to get married – and I suppose I just followed her.' He looked at McVitie guardedly. 'Why do you ask?'

McVitie shrugged. 'I just wondered.' He patted the pocket where he had tucked away the anonymous letter. 'Well, we'll see what we can do about these letters, but I can't promise much. Let me know if you receive any more, or any type of threat.'

'Yes, of course,' Napier said. He was already reaching for the telephone to call Janet by the time McVitie reached the door.

Chapter Twelve

Taggart sat in the pub tucking into a generous portion of steak and kidney pie and chips with obvious relish, frequently adding fresh dollops of tomato ketchup to the plate.

John leaned over the bar counter, great amusement on his face. 'You look like a cannibal who's just been rescued from an uninhabited island,' he observed. 'Are they starving you that much up there?'

Taggart finished wiping up the last smear of ketchup with a chip and popped it into his mouth. 'I like my meat,' he muttered, turning his attention to a bowl of cocktail biscuits on the bar and cramming a handful of them into his mouth. He looked up at John with a canny wink. 'You'll not be charging me a penalty fee for eating these, will you?'

John glanced over to the escape fund box, smiling. 'No, I think you've paid your dues tonight.'

Taggart continued to munch in silence for a while, finally emptying the bowl. He glanced around the deserted pub. 'It's particularly quiet in here tonight,' he said, conversationally.

'Aye, business is bad,' John agreed. 'But I expect it's the same where you are. I've had one or two people in here saying that they're leaving early. I don't suppose people feel much like staying at a health farm when there's a chance of them getting murdered.' He paused briefly. 'Nasty business.'

Taggart agreed with a toss of his head, gratefully accepting the perfect cue to get down to business. Bartenders were often better sources of gossip than even the Lavinia Jeffreys of the world. 'Did she ever come in here – the girl, Belinda?'

'A few times,' John said with a nod. 'Mostly she came with her father, or sometimes to pick up her brother when he'd had a bit too much to drink. But then her father started bringing in that beautician he was knocking off, and I think she tried to be discreet by staying out of the way.'

'Nice bit of stuff was she? The beautician?' Taggart prompted.

This was man-to-man talk. John leaned further over the bar, lowering his voice to that of a confidential whisper even though there was no one else in the bar to overhear them. 'She was a lovely-looking girl, right enough. The funny thing was how much she looked like his own daughter. Almost like sisters, they were. Now, if you ask me, there's something not quite right about a man who picks up a woman who reminds him of his own daughter. Perhaps it's not surprising that his wife was driven to murder, eh?'

The words brought Janet Napier's little speech to Taggart's mind: 'That's why Not Proven is a sentence in itself, the worst possible verdict.'

A howl of wind from outside echoed around the interior of the pub. The log fire in the inglenook fireplace spluttered fiercely as a fall of soot came down the chimney. There was the faint rattle of heavy raindrops against the window. 'Looks like it's blowing up for a wild night,' John observed.

Taggart pulled his coat around his tracksuit and downed the last drop of whisky in his glass. 'Aye, I'd better get going before it really comes down. Wouldn't be the thing to catch the flu while you're staying at a health farm, would it?' He dropped his glass on to the bar top and headed for the door.

'I'd watch my back if I were you,' John called after him.

Taggart stopped in his tracks and turned, puzzled by the strange remark. He waited for John to explain further.

'The lane back to the health farm – sometimes cars come up it far too fast,' John expanded. 'It can be dangerous – especially on a night like this when visibility is bad.'

'Oh, aye. Thanks for the tip,' Taggart said smiling. He pushed open the door, and, fortified by his meal and three double whiskies, began the long trudge back to the Napier Health Resort.

Slippered feet crept stealthily but purposefully along the darkened corridor towards the thin beam of light which shone from beneath the door of Taggart's room. A loose floorboard creaked and the footsteps stopped abruptly, betraying the furtive nature of the nocturnal journey. Then, after a pause of several seconds, the slippered feet moved forwards again.

Taggart sat in the easy chair beside his bed, clad in his pyjamas and dressing-gown. He glanced up from the book he was reading as the faint sound of the creaking floorboard echoed down the quiet corridor outside. He waited for a few seconds, but hearing no further sound, he returned his full attention to the book.

He had only just settled back into it when there was a faint, furtive tapping on his door. Taggart looked up again, dropping the book on to the bed beside him. 'Come in,' he called out. 'It's not locked.'

He fought to keep the annoyance from showing on his face as the door sighed open and Lavinia Jeffrey crept in, dressed in a filmy lavender-blue nightdress. Although she was ostensibly dressed for bed, Taggart could not help noticing that she was also wearing a fresh coat of full make-up. Lavinia had more on her mind, it would seem, than cosy dining-table chat.

Slightly embarrassed, Taggart pulled his dressing-gown more tightly around his knees. Lavinia closed the door behind her and wafted over towards him, trailing a thin wake of perfume. She perched herself comfortably on his bed without the slightest sign of embarrassment.

'I'm so glad you're not in bed,' Lavinia purred at him. 'I just couldn't sleep with that wind outside and the rain clattering against the window. I feel so much safer with a man around.' She broke off to flutter her eyelashes coquettishly. 'Besides, I've got something for you.' With this she plunged her hand into the low-cut top of her nightdress, deep into the cleavage between her more than ample breasts. Taggart gulped, feeling a lump rising in his throat. He squirmed uncomfortably in his chair.

Lavinia's hand eventually came out clutching a bar of carob, which she thrust towards him. 'I thought you might be feeling a little peckish, so I've brought you a snack. It's made from beans and has no caffeine, so it's quite all right.'

'That's very thoughtful of you,' Taggart murmured, much relieved. He accepted the bar of chocolate substitute and unwrapped it. Taking a small bite, he chewed it experimentally. It tasted absolutely nothing like chocolate, but it wasn't quite as bad as he had feared.

Lavinia took the opportunity to edge along the bed towards him. 'I don't know about you, but I can't stop myself thinking about this horrible murder. It could be anyone right here in this building, do you realise that?' She held out her hand towards him. 'My nerves are all jangled up. Feel my hand, it's quite trembly.'

Taggart declined the offer. 'I can quite believe it, Mrs Jeffrey,' he muttered cautiously.

Lavinia sidled another few inches up the bed. 'Oh, do call me Lavinia, please, Jim.' She flashed him another flirtatious smile. 'I always think that staying in a health farm's rather like being at sea. We're all in the same boat together – and besides, I feel like we're old friends already, even though I've only known you a couple of days.' She fluttered her eyelashes again. 'You have a very strong presence, Jim – did anyone ever tell you that? It has a very comforting effect on a woman.'

Taggart found himself wishing that he could have a comforting effect on himself. He had never been much of a ladies' man, even in his younger days – and was extremely limited in experience when it came to middle-aged *femmes fatales*. 'Well . . . Lavinia, this is all very cosy,' he muttered uncomfortably. 'But do you think we should really be doing this?'

The woman had moved as far up the bed as was possible. She was almost sitting in his lap now. She giggled like a schoolgirl. 'I'm sure I don't know what you can be suggesting, Jim. Doing what, exactly?'

'Eating?' Taggart suggested hopefully, waving the carob bar in the air as though it were some sort of magic talisman of protection.

Lavinia leaned against the side of his chair, gazing up at him with smouldering eyes. 'We must all satisfy our appetites, Jim – whatever they are,' she breathed huskily. 'And I'm a woman of insatiable appetite, believe me.'

Taggart did, fervently. He had little doubt that Lavinia Jeffrey could make a Tyrannosaurus Rex look like an over-fed gerbil. The immediate problem was how to avoid being the next meal.

Salvation came like an answer to a prayer, with a loud knock on the door. Lavinia jumped like a galvanised frog, moving at least three feet up the bed. Taggart hastily slid the carob bar back into the wrapper and stuffed it under the mattress. He glanced towards the door, a trapped, guilty look on his face. 'Come in,' he called uncertainly.

Janet Napier walked into the room. Her face, already looking worried, fell even further as she saw Lavinia Jeffrey perched on Taggart's bed. 'I'm sorry, I didn't realise . . .' she stammered, awkwardly. She was already starting to back towards the door again.

Taggart seized the opportunity to take control of the situation once again. 'Mrs Jeffrey was just going,' he said firmly. 'She saw my light on and just wanted some-one to chat to.'

Lavinia, who had been quite prepared to sit there and brazen it out, was totally out-manoeuvred, and had the good grace to accept it. She rose to her feet, smiling politely at Janet Napier. 'That's right, Dr Napier. You haven't interrupted anything.' She looked down at Taggart, keeping the smile fixed on her face even though her eyes were flashing fire. 'Well, I'll see you at breakfast, then.' It sounded almost like a threat. With admirable dignity under the circumstances, she swept out of the room.

Taggart half-smiled at Janet Napier sheepishly. 'I'm a popular man tonight, it seems.'

Janet nodded. 'Obviously.' She sat stiffly on the bed, looking a little out of her depth. It was clear that she was embarrassed and not sure of herself, Taggart realised.

'Finding it hard to sleep?' he asked, trying to help her.

Janet seemed to relax slightly. She was silent for a moment, marshalling her thoughts. 'I was thinking about what you said earlier – about all of us making mistakes in our careers,' she murmured finally. 'The truth is, I *did* make one – twenty years ago, in South Africa.'

127

Taggart's face was calm and reassuring. She obviously wanted to confide in him, and the last thing he wanted to do now was to put her off. 'Why are you telling me this?' he asked gently.

Janet took a deep breath. 'Because it's possible that it has something to do with Belinda's death,' she blurted out. She looked up into Taggart's face again, seeking the understanding she needed to carry on and finding it. 'It was when I was a young doctor in East London,' she went on, 'a town in South Africa, on the coast.'

'And something happened there?' Taggart prompted.

Janet nodded. 'I'd only emigrated out there a few months previously, having gone out to take up a job as an intern in a small local hospital. Then I met Gerald,' she continued. 'We were very much in love, believe it or not. Anyway, we'd decided to get married and Gerald had invited me on a safari. It was supposed to be a sort of pre-honeymoon holiday.'

'Sounds romantic,' Taggart murmured.

'It also sounded very exciting at the time,' Janet went on. 'Perhaps it was that which made me careless, I don't know. The fact is that a ten-year-old girl was admitted into the hospital the day before I was due to go. Her name was Rhona Helliwell. It seemed simple enough. I diagnosed diabetes and gave her an injection of insulin. It was an overdose. She died. There was an enquiry, and the hospital terminated my contract. I flew back to England a few days later and Gerald came to join me as soon as he could close up his own business.' Janet fell silent, staring fixedly at the floor.

Taggart digested the story carefully for a moment.

'And how do you think this affects Belinda?' he asked finally.

Janet raised her eyes to meet his. 'The girl's father made threats against me,' she told him. 'That's why I left so quickly. And of course, when I married Gerald I obviously changed my name – from Lethbridge to Napier – and assumed that was the end of it.'

'But something happened to change that?' Taggart suggested, reading between the lines.

Janet nodded. She held out the book which she had been clutching tightly ever since she entered the room. 'This happened,' she said flatly, handing it to him.

Taggart took the book, noting the photograph of Janet on the back cover. He turned it over and read the title: *The Lethbridge Diet*. It all started to fall into place. 'You published this under your maiden name. Why did you do that, Dr Napier?'

She shrugged. 'Vanity, perhaps. I suppose I just wanted to be recognised for something a little bit more important than treating overweight ladies on a health farm.' Janet reached out to take the book back from Taggart's hands. Opening it, she withdrew an envelope which had been tucked inside and pulled out the single sheet of paper it contained. 'Anyway, the first thing was this – about three weeks after the book was first published.'

She handed the letter over. Taggart read the crudely written message: 'Bloody Murderess.'

'And now this,' Janet went on, wretchedly. 'My daughter for his.' She looked up at Taggart with a frightened, pleading expression. 'Do people really harbour insane grudges like that?'

Taggart nodded gravely. 'Yes, I'm afraid they some-times do, Dr Napier,' he told her sadly.

He was only confirming what she already suspected, but Janet shook her head distractedly, as though she could not bring herself to believe it. 'But to wait so long . . . why?'

Taggart was silently thoughtful for a while. That aspect bothered him as well. 'Tell me, Dr Napier. When did the child die in South Africa?' he asked, finally.

'It was just before Christmas, I remember that.' Janet thought for a few seconds, getting the exact date right in her mind. 'Yes, it was December the twenty-third.' Even as she spoke, she came to the same realisa-tion as Taggart. 'December twenty-third,' she repeated, in a whisper.

Taggart nodded. 'Exactly the same date as the murder of Caroline Kemp,' he muttered grimly, slipping another piece of the bizarre jigsaw puzzle into place.

Janet shuddered suddenly, staring into Taggart's face with real terror showing in her eyes.

Chapter Thirteen

Jardine had been hovering around Jackie Reid's desk for at least five minutes, fidgeting nervously and looking like a little boy with a guilty secret. Finally, tiring of the distraction, she looked up from the reports she had been trying to type out with a little sigh of exasperation. 'Did you want something, Michael?' she enquired.

Jardine looked even more guilty and furtive. He beetled his eyebrows, jerking his head faintly from side to side in what he fondly imagined was a discreet gesture to signal that he wanted a word in private.

Jackie merely looked puzzled, failing to understand his rather unorthodox form of sign language. 'Have you got something wrong with your neck?' she asked, with the faintest trace of concern in her voice.

Jardine flashed her an exasperated glance, rolling his eyes wildly from side to side.

Jackie frowned, beginning to find it all vaguely irritating. She pushed the typewriter away and sat back in her chair, looking up at him with a somewhat exaggerated expression of strained patience. 'Look, I don't know if we're supposed to be playing silly guessing games, but I have got rather a lot of work to do,' she pointed out.

Jardine gave up. Rolling his eyes heavenward, he slunk back to his own desk and picked up the telephone. He dialled Jackie's extension number. When she answered, he cupped his hands around the mouthpiece and hissed into it in a conspiratorial whisper. 'It's me, Michael. Can't you see I need to speak to you – outside the office, in private?' He looked across to Jackie's desk as she turned in his direction, making more awkward jerks of his head towards the outer corridor.

Jackie glared at him across the office. Dropping the telephone back into its rest, she pushed her chair back and stood up, facing him. 'Oh, Michael,' she called out across the room in a loud voice. 'Can I just have a quiet word with you outside for a minute?'

Turning away from her desk, she walked out towards the rest rooms. Jardine caught up with her in the corridor outside. 'What are you doing?' he hissed, looking extremely agitated. 'Couldn't you see I was trying to be discreet?'

Jackie gave him a pitying smile. 'Oh, is that what it was?' I thought you were auditioning for a part in the next James Bond film. Now what's all this cloak and dagger stuff about?'

Jardine grabbed her by the arm and propelled her further down the corridor. 'It's Taggart,' he confided. 'He wants to see us – now.' He broke off to consult his watch. 'Can't you take an early lunch break or something?'

Jackie still couldn't understand the need for all the secrecy and underhand dealing. 'So why don't we both just pick up our notebooks and go?' she wanted to know.

Jardine looked up and down the corridor anxiously, even though there was no one else in sight. His voice dropped to a secretive whisper again. 'Taggart's not officially on this case – remember? This has to be strictly on the QT.'

Jackie shrugged. 'So? Who's to know where we're going? Unless we choose to make a public announcement, we could be doing anything.'

This simple logic brought Jardine back to reality with a bump. Forced to think about it, Jardine realised she was right. He was getting paranoid, he told himself. He relaxed, looking rather sheepish. 'Right – I'll just go and pick up my notebook, then,' he said. 'I'll meet you out in the carpark in two minutes. Don't forget to bring a towel.'

Jackie was confused again. 'Towel?'

Jardine nodded. 'Apparently he's in the steam room.'

Jardine and Jackie walked along the long row of steam cabinets, each one topped with an apparently disembodied human head like something out of a sci-fi horror movie. They eventually identified Taggart, the top of his head swathed in a hot, steaming towel. His red, sweaty face looked for all the world like an overripe tomato perched on top of an oven.

'What kept you so long?' Taggart grumbled. 'I'm cooking in here.'

'Sorry, sir,' Jardine apologised. 'But we had to find an excuse to leave the office. Now, what did you want to see us about?'

Taggart launched into a brief re-cap of the information he had gleaned from Janet Napier. Halfway through, he broke off and swivelled his head in Jackie's direction. 'Don't you think you ought to be taking some notes or something?' he complained.

She looked questioningly across at Jardine, who shrugged briefly and then nodded his head. Receiving this apparent approval, Jackie took out her notebook and a pen.

Satisfied, Taggart carried on. 'Now, I've done a little bit of preliminary digging for you, but you'll have to do the rest for yourselves,' he told them. 'I'm a little restricted in what I can do in this place.'

'I'd say you were totally restricted, sir,' Jackie said, glancing down at the enclosing steam-box and unable to resist the facetious comment. Taggart glared at her. 'Sorry, sir.' Jackie forced a straight face and held her pencil poised over the pad in a business-like fashion.

'Now, the family name is Helliwell,' Taggart went on. 'Scottish origins, from somewhere around the Borders, I believe – before they emigrated to South Africa – down Kelso way.'

Jardine was looking very dubious about all this

information. 'You're talking a heck of a long shot here, sir,' he pointed out. 'And besides, The Biscuit was pretty adamant about you not being involved.'

This bitter reminder caused Taggart to frown. 'Maybe not – but you two are,' he emphasised.

Jackie finished making her notes. She looked as unhappy about it all as Jardine. 'But if we lie about where this information came from . . .'

'Then don't lie,' Taggart snapped, cutting off her objection.

Jardine looked extremely confused about the whole business. 'I just wish I knew who I was actually working for,' he muttered miserably.

Taggart's eyes twinkled impishly. 'It must be as hot out there for you as it is in here for me,' he observed with a grin.

It was hot all right! McVitie's face was almost as red as Taggart's had been in the steam cabinet. He scanned the information from Taggart for a second time before turning on Jardine angrily. 'Did I not make myself quite clear?' he thundered. 'I am conducting this investigation, not Chief Inspector Taggart. And you will take your orders from *me*, and only me – do you hear that?'

Jardine cringed slightly under the verbal assault. He glanced nervously aside at Jackie for support. With a slight gulp, she attempted to come to the rescue, using the carefully thought-out strategy they had both prepared.

'With respect, sir – it was you who asked us to take a statement from Chief Inspector Taggart,' she pointed out. 'And this is the statement he gave us.'

Jardine jumped in quickly with the second line of defence. 'So in the light of what's in that statement, sir – we thought we ought to act on it.'

'Or at least follow it up, sir,' Jackie added, pressing home their temporary advantage.

The stratagem worked perfectly. Barring a slight grunt, McVitie was completely lost for words. His eyes flicked from Jardine's face to Jackie's then back again, his brows contorting into a frown as he tried to figure out exactly how he had been led into the trap. Facial muscles under the surface of his skin twitched with frustration. Finally he gave another grunt, shuddered, and stormed away back to the sanctuary of his private office.

Jackie looked at Jardine, grinning with relief. 'Do you think that means carry on?' she enquired sweetly.

Jardine was triumphant. 'I think that was a direct order,' he said.

Chapter Fourteen

Jardine replaced the telephone and turned towards Jackie. He looked very pleased with himself. 'Well, it does begin to look as though Taggart may have put us on to something after all,' he announced,

Jackie nodded towards the phone. 'Who were you talking to?'

'Hoekestra Copper Company in East London.'

'London?' Jackie couldn't see the connection.

Jardine enlightened her. 'East London, South Africa,' he explained. 'It was the company which first employed Malcolm Helliwell when he emigrated out there. I learned a couple of rather interesting facts.'

'Which were?' Jackie prompted impatiently, fearing that Jardine was about to start winding her up. He had that smug look on his face, she thought. The look he invariably adopted when he was about to tease her with little unfinished snippets of information and vague hints and clues until she was almost twitching with frustration. It was one of his less endearing traits.

However, it seemed he was prepared to be a little more forthcoming on this one. 'Our Mr Helliwell was something of a nutter, it seems,' Jardine went on. 'The copper company sacked him after only a few months because he was a bit of a hot-head – prone to fly off the handle, get into fights, that sort of thing. He also, apparently, had the habit of suddenly deciding to develop a grudge against someone and then persecute them with a long series of underhand attacks. The crunch came when he slipped a poisonous snake into the charge-hand's lunch tin because of an overtime dispute.'

It was all fascinating stuff, Jackie thought, although she couldn't really see where the punchline was coming from. 'But if they sacked him, surely that's the end of the trail?' she queried.

Jardine shook his head. 'I had a bit of luck there. There was one employee of the company who kept in touch with Helliwell after he left. A guy named Henderson, who managed to get on with him, for some reason. They weren't close friends, but they stayed drinking buddies right up to the time his daughter died. It was Henderson I was just talking to.'

Now things were definitely getting more promising. Jackie sucked at her teeth reflectively. 'Which is the time we're interested in,' she observed.

Jardine nodded. 'Right! Now, apparently Helliwell went completely off the rails at this point,' he expanded. 'He went around telling everyone that he had sworn to kill our Dr Janet Napier – or Dr Lethbridge as she was then.'

So far, it all seemed to fit in with Taggart's theory, although there was one aspect which Jackie found hard to fathom. 'But if it was Dr Napier he wanted to kill – why would he wait for over twenty years and then murder her daughter instead?'

Jardine could only shrug. 'If we could understand the minds of psychopaths, our job would probably be a lot easier,' he observed. 'So let's assume that he just thought it was some kind of twisted revenge.'

Jackie shuddered, thinking about it. 'Ugh, twisted is right – like a corkscrew!'

'Anyway, the really important thing from our point of view is that Helliwell also came back to Scotland with his wife and son shortly afterwards,' Jardine went on. 'He bought a farm or a smallholding somewhere in the Borders.'

'Somewhere? That means we don't have an address?' Jackie queried.

Jardine didn't seem too worried. 'Just be thankful that his name was Helliwell and not Smith,' he said.

Somehow, Jackie knew what was coming, but she asked anyway. 'And why should I be thankful?'

Jardine grinned at her. 'Because you're the one who is going to start looking for him,' he told her, confirming her fears.

'That could take ages,' Jackie complained, but it carried no ice with Jardine in his present mood.

'So take ages,' he said, generously. 'You've got all afternoon.'

Gerald Napier took one more sad and lingering look at the photograph of Belinda on his consulting-room desk. It was virtually all he had done that afternoon, apart from seeing one patient with nicotine-stained fingers who complained about a bad cough. He had not received a very sympathetic bedside manner.

Napier slid his chair back and pushed himself to his feet. It was time to go, back to the loneliness of the flat. Thinking about it depressed him even more. Perhaps he should have made more of an effort to accept Janet's innocence, he thought. At least he would have had the health farm to fall back on now, when he desperately needed something to occupy his mind. It was all too late now, of course. Belinda's death had probably snapped whatever threads of family life still remained up to that point. Janet would have thrown what was left of her emotions into Jeremy, leaving him with nothing, not even a viable private practice.

Napier closed and locked his filing cabinet and trudged heavily towards the door. Outside, in the reception area, Agnes Pollock was still finding something to keep her busy, cross-referencing the record files of private patients with past health farm guests on the computer database.

Napier glanced at his watch. It was nearly six o'clock. 'Get yourself home, Agnes,' he chided gently. 'You've done more than your fair share today.'

She looked up at him, with a patient, almost long-suffering expression on her face. 'If it's all the same to you, Dr Napier, I'll stay on for a while yet. I thought I'd get a list of past health farm patients and send them a little reminder letter to let them know we're still in

140

private practice. Who knows – perhaps we can get a few patients back.'

She seemed set on the idea, and Napier was in no mood to stay and argue with her. Besides, it was a good idea, and might just work. The way things were going, anything was worth trying. He nodded, crossing to the coat rack and putting on his topcoat. 'Well, just don't stay on too long,' he told her. 'Good night, then.'

'Good night, Dr Napier.' Agnes watched him fondly as he walked out of the door.

Janet was standing on the front step as he opened the outer door, poised with her finger in the air, just about to ring the bell. The surprise encounter caught them both unawares. There was an awkward silence for several seconds.

'I wasn't sure you'd still be here,' Janet said finally, uncertainly. 'I thought it was time we talked.'

Now that the initial shock of seeing her was over, Napier felt glad she was there. Perhaps, after all, there might still be a meeting point between them. He gave her his first genuine smile in two days. 'I'm glad you're here,' he murmured. 'Do you want to come in, or would you rather go somewhere else?'

Janet was already stepping over the threshold. 'Here is fine,' she said. Sliding past him, she made her own way through to the reception office.

Agnes Pollock looked up from her work as Janet entered. She found it impossible to cover up her own look of surprise with a feigned smile. 'Good evening, Dr Napier,' she said, with cool politeness.

'Hello, Agnes.' Janet walked straight past her and into Gerald's consulting room. She sat herself down as

141

he followed her in and closed the door.

Napier seated himself at his desk, facing her. They stared at each other for a few moments, each waiting for the other to break the deadlock of embarrassment.

Finally, Janet sighed. 'The police think that Caroline was murdered by mistake,' she said. 'Because she had borrowed Belinda's car that night.'

Napier nodded his head. 'Yes, I know what the police think.'

Janet looked at him with a slightly puzzled expression. He didn't seem to get the point she was trying to make. 'But don't you see what that means, Gerald? Belinda was the intended victim from the start. It means that I wasn't guilty, Gerald – unless you want to believe that I would want to harm our own daughter.'

Napier looked stunned for a moment. Then a bitter, accusing look formed on his face. 'My God,' he muttered, under his breath. 'How can you be so utterly selfish? Our daughter is dead and all you can think of is your reputation.' He jumped up from his desk and began pacing fretfully around the room.

His anger took Janet aback for a moment, until she seemed to realise that she was being accused all over again. All the pent-up frustrations and turmoil of the past months erupted in a wave of defensive rage. 'I went through hell!' she blazed at him. 'Have you any idea what it was like?'

Napier stopped his pacing. He turned to stare her in the eyes, suddenly calmer. 'Do you think it was any easier for me?' he demanded. 'Don't you know that a day didn't pass when I didn't curse myself for *not* being able to believe in your innocence? There are all sorts of hells, Janet.'

Janet saw the anguish on his face. He was right, of course. He had lost so much. She moved towards him, reaching out to wrap her arm around his shoulder. She glanced down at the photograph of Belinda on his desk. 'Poor Gerald,' she murmured. 'She was so special to you, wasn't she?'

Napier shuddered as a wave of emotion rippled through him. He reached down to the desk, brushing his fingertips over the surface of the framed photograph. 'Belle of the Ball,' he breathed huskily. 'Do you remember when we first called her that?'

Janet nodded sadly, sniffing back the tears. 'I remember. It was her tenth birthday.'

'She'd just put on her very first party dress. She looked so beautiful, so grown up,' Napier went on. He fell silent, gazing at Belinda's picture and taking comfort from Janet's embrace.

'Shall we go to the funeral tomorrow together?' Janet asked gently, after a while.

Napier nodded. 'Of course,' he murmured.

Janet squeezed him, lifting her hand to run her fingers through his hair. It felt good, better than she remembered. Beneath her sadness, there were the first stirrings of hope in all those bitter months. Her daughter was gone forever, but at least she had her husband back again. She kissed him lightly on the side of his face. 'We'll get over this somehow,' she promised him.

'And Jeremy?' Napier asked doubtfully. The relationship between the two of them had always been a strained one, even in easier times.

Janet spoke for her son. 'He'll come round,' she

assured Gerald. 'We'll be a family again – you'll see.'

Napier tried hard to believe her. He desperately *wanted* to believe her. His eyes fell on Belinda's picture again. 'But not a whole family,' he thought to himself, bitterly. No matter what happened, they could never be a whole family again.

Chapter Fifteen

Janet had left. Napier would have liked to have gone with her, but it wasn't really practical, he realised. He had moved all his clothes to the flat, so he would have to return there to change for the funeral in the morning anyway. And perhaps it was best to take things slowly, one step at a time. Reconciliation was not something which could be rushed. It was only partings which were carried out in haste.

For the second time that evening, he got ready to leave. Agnes was on the telephone as he walked into reception. She waved her hand in the air, attracting his attention and gesturing for him to hold on a while. Napier waited patiently as she finished the call.

'That was Mrs Drake,' she announced as she

replaced the receiver. 'She would like you to make a house call, if you don't mind.'

Napier ran the name through his memory, forming a mental picture of Mrs Drake. 'I thought she was staying out at the health resort?'

'She was,' Agnes told him. 'Until yesterday. But all the police activity upset her and she left early. Now she's been taken rather poorly and she'd like you to visit her at this address.' Agnes handed over a slip of paper.

Napier studied it. 'This isn't her address,' he pointed out. 'Mrs Drake has a big house in Goldmere Drive.'

'She's staying with friends, apparently,' Agnes informed him.

Napier clicked his teeth in annoyance. 'It's not an emergency or anything, is it? Can't it wait?'

Agnes looked troubled, torn between her sympathy for him and her concern for the patient. 'She did sound pretty dreadful over the phone,' she pointed out. 'A nasty chest and throat infection.'

Napier swallowed his annoyance. 'All right – I'll go out there as soon as I've had something to eat.' He started to leave again, turning back to Agnes on an afterthought. 'Oh, don't take any appointments tomorrow. The funeral's in the morning and I'll be with my family for the rest of the day.'

'I understand, Dr Napier.' Agnes struggled for some words of sympathy or comfort, but nothing came to mind. She managed only a sad little smile of reassurance.

Napier cruised back down the street for the second time, straining his eyes in the evening gloom to check the house numbers against the address which Agnes had written down on the appointment slip. Finally he stopped the car again outside number 22 and stared at its dark and apparently lifeless exterior through the side window.

It appeared to be empty and deserted, with no sign of light showing from any of the windows. More than that, the detached house looked as though it had been derelict for some considerable time. The small front garden was completely overgrown with weeds and the gate hung drunkenly open on one rusted hinge. Inside it, the driveway was littered with various pieces of debris and rubbish. It hardly looked like the sort of place which Mrs Drake would consider staying in. Nor could Napier imagine her having friends who lived in such squalor. She was such a precise, fussy woman, who had lived most of her life accustomed to the comforts of wealth and servants. Her attitude to the health resort staff clearly established her as a bit of a snob.

Napier flipped on the car's interior light and studied Agnes's note again, in case he had misread her writing. There could be no mistaking her clear, precise print, and it seemed highly unlikely that she would have made a mistake in taking it down. In the two years she had worked for him, Napier had never known the woman to be anything other than the very model of efficiency.

However, there was a first time for everything. Napier snatched up his car phone and punched out Agnes's home number. She answered almost immediately.

'Hello, Agnes? It's Dr Napier. Look, sorry to bother you at home, but are you sure you took that address for Mrs Drake down correctly? It's just that I'm here, and the house seems to be deserted.'

As he spoke, a light suddenly snapped on in one of the upstairs windows. Napier spoke into the phone again, cutting into Agnes's apologetic reply.

'Oh, as you were – it seems there is someone in after all. Sorry again for bothering you.'

He replaced the phone, reached over into the back seat of the car to retrieve his medical bag and got out. Sliding his way through the half-open gate, he made his way towards the front door, nearly tripping over a 'For Sale' sign which appeared to have been ripped down and thrown across the drive. Reaching the front door, Napier was just about to ring the bell when he realised that the door was already slightly open. He pushed it ajar cautiously, poking his head inside.

'Mrs Drake?' he called. There was no answer. Increasingly puzzled, Napier stepped over the portal and into the hall. He called again. 'Anyone at home? It's Dr Napier.'

There was still no reply. He walked further into the hallway, pausing at the foot of the stairs. A faint light shone down from the top landing, and Napier could only assume it was from one of the bedrooms. At the top of the stairs, he could see a large suitcase leaning against the wall. These were the only signs of life, giving Napier no choice but to investigate. It was possible that Mrs Drake's throat infection had worsened to the point where she was incapable of shouting back in answer to his call, Napier reasoned. And, if she was going to be anywhere, she would be upstairs in bed.

He began to climb the stairs. There was a sudden, blood-curdling squeal, and the feel of something squirming beneath his feet which nearly panicked him. With a pounding heart, Napier turned and looked back down the stairs at the fleeing black cat on whose tail he had trodden in the gloom. Taking a deep breath, he continued up the stairs to the fatal landing.

The light came from the half-open door of the front bedroom. Napier made his way along the landing towards it, reaching up to the wall to flick on the first light switch that he came across.

Nothing happened. It was as if the house's power supply was down, for some reason. Napier jiggled the switch a couple of times, logic telling him that there must be electrical power for the bedroom light to work. Perhaps a fuse had blown, or the landing light bulb had gone.

Reaching the bedroom door, he pushed it fully open and peered in. The empty bed was stripped down to the mattress. The light he had seen came from a large flashlight propped up against the headrest. Other than the bed, the room was devoid of furniture . . . except for a small child's chair, placed in the middle of the floor and directly in the beam of the flashlight. And, seated in the chair, a black, life-sized baby doll, dressed in what appeared to be a ball gown. Its glassy eyes glinted in the beam of the torch, staring directly at him as though it had been arranged there especially to confront him.

The entire, bizarre scene appeared to have been set up like a tableau, a scene taken straight off the set of a horror movie. Yet, for all its implied menace, the little scene exercised a morbid fascination. Transfixed by the glinting, hypnotic eyes of the doll, Napier stepped into the room and moved towards it. He bent over to examine the doll more closely. It was old, Napier realised – at least twenty years old. Its cracked, chipped face showed distinct signs of wear and tear, and the material of the blue ball dress it was wearing looking thin and faded. Close up, it did not seem quite so menacing. Napier prodded it tentatively with one finger, the slight movement making the doll's weighted eyes rock up and down in their sockets as though it was about to nod off to sleep. Napier jumped back, totally unprepared for this sudden and unnerving sign of animation. It was as if the accursed thing was alive, he thought.

The thought was to be his last. Behind him, a dark, balaclava-hooded figure moved soundlessly into the room from the darkened hallway outside. An arm rose in the air, the hand at the end of it clutching the short, weighted and balanced handle of an African throwing knife from which jutted three wickedly curved and pointed blades.

The killer's arm flashed downwards. There was a momentary swishing sound as the horrendous weapon was thrown and it sliced through the air towards Napier's back. Then one of the fearsome blades embedded itself heavily between his shoulder-blades, penetrating deep through flesh and muscle until it reached his heart.

Napier died instantly, his only sound a last gasp of air expelled from his lungs by the force of the weapon's impact. He collapsed forwards over the doll and chair, his eyes open but unseeing.

The horror scene was complete now. The killer looked down on it and smiled with satisfaction.

Chapter Sixteen

Jardine sat in the car outside the back of Maryhill Police Station, fuming with impatience and glancing nervously at his watch. The funeral of Belinda Napier was due to start in less than ten minutes and there was still no sign of Jackie Reid.

More to pass the time than anything else, Jardine tilted down the rear-view mirror and used it to adjust the knot of his black tie, which refused to sit quite to his satisfaction. He tugged at it irritably, using it as something upon which to take out his frustrations. He hated black ties anyway, and was never comfortable using a standard knot. It was just that someone, at sometime, had implanted in him the slightly ridiculous idea that a Windsor knot was a little too dressy for a funeral, and it had stuck with him.

Apart from the problems of dressing for the occasion, Jardine had never quite figured out why it was necessary for a police presence at murder victims' funerals anyway. It was hardly a matter of respect, since they spent days questioning relatives and close friends at the very time they most needed to be left alone with their grief. Jardine could only suppose the point of the exercise was to look out for guilty faces amongst the mourners.

He glanced at his watch again and tapped on the car horn impatiently. Perhaps another full minute passed before Jackie finally appeared, sauntering unhurriedly towards the car. Jardine leaned over and opened the passenger door, calling out to her to hurry up. 'Get a move on,' he urged. 'Or are you planning on being late for your own funeral?'

Jackie ignored the sarcasm. She was above all that, knowing that she had an ace up her sleeve. She climbed into the car beside him. 'I take it you're not at all interested in the telephone conversation I just had with the Lothian and Borders police, then?' she asked Jardine with deceptive casualness.

She had his attention at once. Jardine turned on her as he started the car and began to pull out of the station carpark. 'Well, what did you find out?' he demanded impatiently.

'Something very interesting,' Jackie said, taking a leaf from Jardine's book and dangling a carrot under his nose.

But he was in no mood to play games. 'Get to the point,' he snapped irritably.

'I sent out a general communication yesterday on the name Helliwell,' Jackie said, filling in the immediate background. 'And it seems the name rang a bell with a DC McLoughlin in Penicuik. He remembers dealing with the suicide of a Mrs Marjory Helliwell, some years ago. She drowned herself on their farm, near a little village called Cowieslinn.'

It sounded promising, but Jardine remained cautious. 'But is there any reason to suspect that these might be our Helliwells?'

Jackie looked pleased with herself. 'Nothing absolutely positive, but there's strong circumstantial evidence that we're dealing with the same family. The woman – Marjory Helliwell – had apparently been mentally unbalanced for many years, having suffered trauma after the death of her young daughter.'

Jardine was thoughtful for a while. It was getting better and better. 'Okay, so that much fits,' he admitted finally. 'Is there anything else?'

Jackie nodded. 'According to DC McLoughlin, Marjory wasn't the only one with mental problems. Apparently the whole family had the reputation of being a bit peculiar, according to the neighbours. There were several incidents over the years, although for the most part they kept very much to themselves and lived almost like hermits.'

Jardine made an effort to keep the elation from his face as they approached the cemetery gates. 'Could be our man,' he muttered. 'Do we know where he is now?'

'Sorry, that's where the trail breaks down again,' Jackie apologised. 'Helliwell sold the farm soon after his wife's death and moved on. McLoughlin has no idea what happened to him or his son after that. But at least we're a bit closer to him now. It's better than being twenty years behind.'

Jardine slowed the car down to crawling pace as they entered the cemetery. He found a couple of seconds to flash Jackie a congratulatory smile. 'Nice work,' he muttered, in a rare compliment.

Jackie basked in the unaccustomed praise. 'Do I get ten Brownie points this morning?'

'Five,' Jardine allowed her, grudgingly. He pulled the car to a halt behind a hearse and two black limousines. Belinda Napier's coffin was still in the back of the hearse, much to Jardine's relief. 'Looks like we're in time after all,' he observed. 'The funeral seems to have been held up for some reason.' He climbed out of the car and waited for Jackie to join him. Together, they walked slowly over to where Janet and Jeremy Napier stood waiting. They both looked agitated and worried, as though there was something over and above the funeral on their minds.

'Is anything wrong?' Jackie prompted gently.

Jeremy directed his attention to Jardine. 'There's something very wrong. My father hasn't shown up for the funeral. He was supposed to meet us at the house over an hour ago.'

'Have you tried to contact him?' Jardine asked.

Jeremy nodded. 'We've phoned his Glasgow flat and the surgery. There's no answer from his home and his receptionist hasn't seen or heard from him since yesterday evening.'

'Perhaps he's had to go out on an emergency call,'

Jackie suggested. 'He's a doctor, after all.'

Janet Napier stepped forward, shaking her head. 'No, his receptionist would know about something like that.' She paused, renewed worry showing on her face. 'Besides, there is nothing on this earth which would prevent him from coming to Belinda's funeral. He idolised her. She was his life.'

'Then perhaps that's it,' Jardine suggested, clutching at straws. 'Perhaps he just couldn't face the thought of seeing her buried.'

Janet shook her head again. 'I spoke to him last night. It was all arranged. We were coming together – as a family again.'

Jardine thought for a moment. 'Then you were the last person to see him last night?'

'Apart from Agnes, his receptionist,' Janet agreed. 'But I understand she spoke to him on the telephone later on. Some trouble with the address of a house-call he went out to make.'

'Trouble?' Jackie picked up on the word. 'What sort of trouble?'

Janet shrugged distractedly. 'I don't know the details. Agnes Pollock, his receptionist, can probably tell you more than I can.'

Jardine's face betrayed his increasing concern. He fished in his pocket and drew out his notebook and a pen, handing them to Janet. 'Here, write down the address and telephone number of the surgery. We'll go and see if we can find out what's happened.'

Jackie smiled reassuringly at Janet Napier as she scribbled down the details and handed the notepad back to Jardine. 'Don't worry, Dr Napier, I'm sure everything is all right. We'll be back as soon as we can.'

It was a promise she was unable to keep.

'Well, that's Napier's car all right,' Jardine said, checking off the licence number of the car parked outside number 22. He peered into the vehicle and tested the door, which was locked. 'It's locked up and the keys aren't in the ignition,' he pointed out to Jackie. 'That means he must have gone into the house.'

'But apparently didn't come out again,' Jackie put in, stating the obvious. She looked up at Jardine with a worried expression on her face. 'It doesn't look good, does it?'

The implications were obvious, but Jardine tried to make light of them. 'We won't know anything until we go inside and take a look,' he muttered.

Jackie stared at the dilapidated house. Even in broad daylight, it looked slightly menacing. She glanced back at Jardine, uncertainty showing on her face. 'Don't you think we'd better wait for some back-up?'

Jardine dismissed her objection. 'We haven't got time,' he pointed out. 'Anyway, it'll be all right, I'm sure.'

Unconvinced, Jackie followed him hesitantly up the drive towards the front door. It was open, as it had been the previous evening. Jardine pushed it ajar, stepping into the hallway. Jackie followed him in rather more cautiously. She stood just inside the door, looking around apprehensively and sniffing at the air. It was musty and damp – the smell of neglect and decay.

'A house-call? To this place?' she queried, looking up at Jardine uncertainly.

He was beginning to feel uneasy himself, as well as picking up Jackie's bad vibes. A show of male bravado seemed the best way of covering it up. 'Maybe you'd better wait here,' he suggested, somewhat condescendingly. 'I'll check the downstairs rooms first.'

He headed in the direction of the kitchen, leaving Jackie standing by the front door feeling slightly annoyed with herself. Having let her fears show, she had allowed Jardine to slip into his protective male role, and it rankled. There was only one way to reassert herself. She waited until Jardine was out of sight before turning towards the staircase. Then, taking a deep breath, she began to climb the stairs towards the top landing.

She was just coming down again as Jardine finished searching the downstairs rooms and returned to the hallway. He looked up at her, noting the grim expression on her pale face. 'Napier?'

Jackie nodded. 'He's up there. Just like the others.' She paused for a moment to fully recover herself and her professional detachment. 'You'd better get on the car phone to McVitie,' she suggested finally. 'And don't forget to tell him to bring Doc Andrews.'

The doll, chair and flashlight were all gone, along with the murder weapon. There was only Gerald Napier's body, lying stiffly on the bare, uncarpeted floor, most of his back darkly stained with dried, caked blood.

Dr Andrews was getting used to seeing the unusual wounds, but they continued to baffle him. He knelt down beside Napier's corpse, gently probing the area around the wound with a slender wooden spatula.

'The same type of injury?' McVitie asked.

Andrews climbed to his feet, nodding. 'Exactly,' he said firmly. 'There's absolutely no doubt in my mind that we're dealing with the same weapon – although what it might be I can't even hazard a guess.'

'Exactly what is it that you find so baffling about these killings?' Jardine asked. Andrews had never really spelled it out in his presence.

The doctor shrugged. 'Just about everything,' he admitted. 'In all my years in forensic medicine, I've never come across anything quite like it. To make a single wound, this deep and this effective, would take a very special kind of implement. Certainly no ordinary knife of my experience would do it.'

'You made a special mention of the force involved with previous cases,' McVitie put in. 'Any further theories on that aspect?'

Dr Andrews sucked at his teeth reflectively. 'I can only repeat what I said all along. To inflict this wound must have taken terrific force – and great skill. I have to admit that I've never seen killing so neat – if neat is a word you can apply to murder.'

Jardine had been quietly thinking to himself. The germ of a theory was forming in his mind. 'Could that force be explained by some form of propulsion, perhaps?' he asked Andrews.

'Such as a spear, for instance?' Jackie Reid added, following his line of reasoning.

Andrews initially looked dismissive. He smiled somewhat patronisingly at Jackie. 'I think someone walking round Glasgow with a spear would rather attract attention, don't you think?' He fell silent, considering Jardine's suggestion more seriously. The expression on his face changed, to one of possibility. 'But yes, if you were thinking in terms of some sort of heavy *throwing* knife, then that might certainly help to explain it,' he conceded at last. 'But as I said, it would take a great deal of skill.'

McVitie was feeling a bit out of things. 'Spears,' he muttered scathingly. 'We'll be talking about marauding Zulus next. Or demented circus knife-throwers.' He shot Jackie Reid a withering glance. 'Can we get back to facts, and not wild theories?'

Jackie gulped, shrinking into herself. 'Sorry, sir. Just trying to be helpful.'

McVitie took advantage of her ensuing silence to advance his own interpretation of events. 'No, if you ask me, whoever lured Gerald Napier here had to know this woman Drake's voice well enough to impersonate her. Also that she was a patient of his. To me that all suggests someone at the health farm. An employee, perhaps, or one of the other guests.'

'With what motive, sir?' Jardine asked.

It was a polite enough enquiry, but McVitie bristled. 'Any one of a dozen reasons,' he snapped testily. 'A personal grudge against the Napiers? Some crank with a bee in his bonnet about health farms? Probably nothing whatsoever to do with this man Helliwell, or the dubious South African connection.' He was well into his stride now, having regained the initiative. It seemed politic to quit while he was ahead. McVitie turned towards the door as he delivered his parting shot. 'This isn't a case for inspired guesswork,' he said emphatically. 'Just simple, solid, police detection. Old-fashioned legwork.'

Chapter Seventeen

Taggart's face was a mask of indignant rage. 'Legwork!' he roared, spitting out the single word. 'What does that man know about legwork? His have been tucked under a desk for so long he's forgotten what they look like, let alone what they're for!'

Jardine stood back slightly, giving Taggart his head. It was obvious that the man's frustration was beginning to tell on him, and Jardine could understand it. To have a juicy case like this one going on right under his nose and not be a part of it must gall him beyond belief. Equally obvious was the fact that Taggart's imposed sabbatical was not doing him any good at all. Far from being a rest cure, it seemed to be having the opposite effect. Taggart was now exhibiting greater signs of stress than he had before he came in to the health farm.

Jardine waited patiently until the man had apparently simmered down a little. 'Anyway, I just thought I'd come out here and fill you in with what's going on,' he explained. 'Perhaps that was a mistake.'

Taggart's angry face cleared slightly. 'No, I'm grateful, Michael,' he said in a calmer voice. 'I'm glad you did. Sorry if I'm acting like a bear with a sore head.'

Jardine was quite taken aback. An apology of any sort from Taggart was a rarity, but a contrite apology was really something else. Perhaps he had been wrong, Jardine thought. Perhaps the rest was doing some good after all.

They continued strolling round the grounds of the health resort for a while in contemplative silence.

'So, what was the name of this patient that Gerald Napier supposedly went to visit?' Taggart asked, finally.

'A Mrs Drake,' Jardine told him. 'She was staying here at the health farm until the other day.'

Taggart nodded thoughtfully. 'Aye, I saw her. Strange woman. I assume someone has checked her out.'

'The Biscuit went to see her himself,' Jardine confirmed. 'There's no question of any involvement on her part, apparently. She spent the entire evening at the opera with a group of friends and stayed the night with them. All good, solid citizens, including an ex-chief inspector. A perfect alibi, it would appear. Oh, and no cough,' Jardine added on afterthought. 'Napier's receptionist said that the person who telephoned had a nasty cough and croaky voice. The real Mrs Drake spoke like a walking advert for throat lozenges.'

Taggart digested the information philosophically.

He had expected no less. For all her strange appearance, there was no way he could see Mrs Drake as a knife-wielding maniac.

They approached the front of the mansion house. There were at least three taxis parked in the drive outside the front door, and much activity as people bustled in and out of the building carrying suitcases. The traffic was strictly one-way, Jardine noted. 'Looks like a lot of people are leaving,' he observed.

Taggart nodded in agreement. 'Aye – death isn't a very good advertisement for a health farm,' he muttered sadly. 'There are already rumours flying about that Janet Napier might be thinking about closing the place down.'

He sounded quite upset at the prospect, Jardine thought, somewhat surprised. 'Thought you'd be looking forward to getting back to work, sir,' he said.

Taggart looked at him miserably. 'Oh I am, Michael, I am, believe me. But can you see The Biscuit letting me back on this case? He'll insist I take the rest of my leave, you mark my words.'

'So what's so bad about that?' Jardine wanted to know. He couldn't understand Taggart's depression.

Taggart stopped in his tracks, staring at Jardine with a look of shock on his face. 'Are you kidding, Michael? Can you see me painting a kitchen ceiling?'

Thinking about it, Jardine had to admit that it was not an easy mental picture to conjure up. There was not much he could say to reassure the man. He lapsed into silence as Taggart started walking again.

They passed a group of overweight ladies exercising on the lawn under the direction of Ian Gowrie. Recognising Taggart, Lavinia Jeffrey broke off from her physical jerks to wave to him enthusiastically. Flushing with embarrassment, Taggart raised his hand and acknowledged her with a vague flutter. 'My dining companion,' he muttered self-consciously to Jardine, by way of explanation.

Jardine grinned. 'Looks like you created a big impression with your table manners, sir.'

Taggart scowled at him. 'Mention a word of this to DC Reid and I'll have your guts for garters,' he threatened. He paused, thinking about her. 'What's she doing, by the way?'

'As much as she can,' Jardine told him. 'It's very awkward, sir. The Biscuit is watching us both like a hawk. I only found an excuse to get out here because there are still a couple of guests we haven't taken statements from yet.'

Taggart looked glum. 'I understand,' he muttered. 'Has she managed to get any further with this Helliwell business?'

Jardine nodded. 'She's managed to track down the woman psychiatrist who treated Helliwell's wife. She practises in Edinburgh now.'

'Probably where she's most needed,' Taggart said cynically. 'Have either of you managed to have a word with her yet? She could have access to the very information we need.'

Jardine shook his head apologetically. 'As I said, sir – The Biscuit's watching us both like a hawk. He doesn't want us to pursue the Helliwell connection at all.'

Taggart screwed up his face in frustration. 'That man's always looking for some nice simple explanation,' he complained. 'He won't even consider what's right under his nose.'

Jardine was thoughtful for a while. 'With respect, sir – McVitie could be right,' he pointed out, playing Devil's Advocate. 'All the clues so far do tend to point the finger at someone here at the health farm. Someone in a position to know the movements of the Napier family, someone known well enough to them to get close without arousing suspicion. Belinda Napier would hardly have stopped her car in an isolated spot in the middle of the night for a stranger. And, in Gerald Napier's case, this someone would have had to know about Mrs Drake to use her as a lure.'

Taggart gave the argument a few seconds of consideration, finally rejecting it with an emphatic shake of his head. 'No, I'm right on this one, Michael – I know I'm right. The motive's just not there, not for a sustained vendetta like this.'

It was exactly this point which formed the core of Jardine's own doubts about McVitie's theory. Now, confronting them, he felt awkward, trapped and confused between two strong arguments. For although Taggart would have bristled at the comparison, he and McVitie were actually very much alike. They both held fierce personal convictions, and were both equally adamant about others accepting them. Making a choice between the two could only be a gut decision, based on instinct rather than logic. But then Jardine's personal experience of Taggart had to give the man the edge. On balance, his hunches were right many more times than they were wrong. And this one seemed particularly strong.

Taggart was studying his colleague's troubled face,

seeing the clash of interests there. 'You're not sure, are you, Michael,' he asked, with uncharacteristic gentleness. 'Go with me on this one – please.'

It was the humility of this direct appeal which finally swung the balance. Jardine couldn't remember the last time he had heard Taggart use the word 'please'. It was just not in his normal vocabulary. In a way, it seemed to encapsulate the man's sense of desperation.

'It's not going to be easy,' Jardine murmured uncertainly. 'If McVitie finds out, he'll throw the book at us.'

The brief look of triumph which flashed across Taggart's face was quickly replaced by one of conspiratorial cunning. 'The Biscuit ordered you to interview all previous health farm clients, didn't he?' he asked.

Jardine agreed with a faint shrug, looking a little puzzled. 'Yes, but I don't see how that's going to help, though.'

Taggart's eyes glittered. 'Some of those people probably live in Edinburgh, wouldn't you think?' he suggested.

Jardine finally caught on. 'And some of them might live not a million miles away from a certain psychiatrist.'

Taggart grinned, slapping Jardine on the back. 'That's my boy, Michael,' he said, managing to make it sound like the highest possible commendation. 'I knew you wouldn't let me down.'

Even though he had committed himself, Jardine could still not quite believe the ease and subtlety with which it had been achieved. He regarded Taggart with an expression of disbelief mixed with awe. 'Someday we'll swing for you, sir,' he said ruefully. He glanced down at his watch. 'Well, as I'm still working for two bosses, I guess I'd better get back to it.' He turned back towards the house and began to walk towards the car.

Taggart dawdled behind him, watching Jardine's departing back with a faint smile of satisfaction playing on his lips. He felt slightly guilty about manipulating him in the way he had, but there really wasn't much choice. If he was to stay in the ball game – albeit in only a vicarious role – then using Jardine and Jackie Reid was his only option.

Taggart gazed over to the front of the house, where another three or four cars had arrived to take away departing guests. It was starting to look like a full-scale evacuation, he realised. A complete shut-down must now be a distinct possibility – and this thought evoked mixed feelings.

On the one hand, he would not be too upset to leave the resort. The trouble with health, Taggart had decided, was that you could get too much of it. He'd been steamed and starved, prodded and pummelled and immersed in everything from hot mud to iced water. His body must be in better condition than it had been for years – but it was his mind which was now getting flabby. Above all else, Taggart wanted to get his brain active again. He was itching to get back to work. With Jardine and Jackie's help, he could at least stay in touch with the situation until he was in a position to do so, and he already had a few ideas on that score.

On the downside, of course, the closure of the health farm might take the Napier case out of his jurisdiction. If Janet Napier was forced out of business and had to move away, it was possible that the vengeful killer would be appeased, leaving a string of unsolved murders which would moulder in McVitie's files forever. Or the whole case would simply move on to someone else's patch. Taggart found both possibilities equally unpalatable.

Dr Janet Napier was also watching the departing guests from an upstairs window with a sinking heart. It seemed that everything was being stolen away from her piece by piece. First her family, and now the business she and Gerald had spent half a lifetime building up.

Sadly, she turned away from the window and crossed the drawing-room to where Jeremy sat on the chesterfield sifting through a large bundle of letters. 'More bad news?' Janet asked, already sensing the answer.

Her son nodded forlornly. 'Twelve more advance bookings cancelled today,' he announced. 'And four new guests who were due to book in this morning just didn't bother to show up.'

Janet sighed deeply. 'It hardly seems worth staying open after this week,' she observed miserably.

Jeremy tried to console her. 'Perhaps it's just a temporary thing,' he offered. 'Business will pick up again just as soon as all the publicity dies down. People have short memories.'

Janet was unconvinced. 'Some people do,' she muttered under her breath, with heavy irony. Jeremy didn't understand. He wasn't really meant to. She waved her hand vaguely around in the air, taking in not just the room but the whole building. 'This was our dream, your father and I,' she murmured distantly. 'You wouldn't believe that we had dreams once.'

Jeremy said nothing, sensing that his mother needed to voice her thoughts aloud. She wasn't even really talking to him, he realised.

'Do you remember when you were just a little boy, and you were so afraid of the dark?' Janet asked suddenly.

The question seemed to have no significance at all, but it begged some sort of a response. Jeremy nodded. 'Yes, I remember,' he said, in little more than a whisper.

'Sometimes we're all afraid of the dark,' Janet went on. 'Sometimes we have good reason to be.' She was silent and thoughtful for several moments, a misty, faraway look coming into her eyes. 'The darkest dark I ever knew was once when your father took me away on a safari. I remember that one night we sat out on the veranda of the house we were staying in and listened to the sounds in the still air. There were the calls of jackals and hyenas – screaming and yelling as they hunted for their prey. I was frightened. Your father took me in his arms and he hugged me. "There's madness in the night," he said.'

Janet broke off from her reverie abruptly, the vacant look in her eyes suddenly replaced by sheer terror. She moved across to her son, reaching down to grip his shoulders. She was shaking uncontrollably. 'Who's out there, Jeremy?' she asked desperately, hopelessly. 'What madness is in the night now?'

Jeremy rose slowly to his feet, taking his mother in his arms to offer her what little physical comfort he could.

She relaxed in his embrace for a while, then suddenly tensed and pulled away. Her face was set and firm

169

again, her tone strong and decisive as if she had tapped a new source of strength deep within herself. 'We're going to close down, Jeremy,' she announced with finality. 'I want to go abroad where nobody knows who I am and I never want to see this place again.'

Jeremy looked shell-shocked. Seeing the look on his face, Janet smiled at him understandingly. 'Don't worry. There will be enough left over from the sale of this place to provide for your future.'

Jeremy shook his head. 'It wasn't that. I was just thinking that I feel sort of responsible.'

Janet frowned. 'Responsible? Why?'

Jeremy looked sheepish. 'I've never really been much use here, have I? As long as my bank balance has been healthy, I never took much interest.'

Janet regarded him fondly. 'You supported me throughout the trial. And since. I'll never forget that,' she told him.

He seemed to take some comfort from her words. Pulling himself up with a new sense of self-confidence, he stared her directly in the eyes. 'You're quite sure about this, aren't you?'

Janet nodded. 'It's the first thing I've felt really sure about for the past three months,' she replied.

'All right. I'll tell all the staff and make all the necessary preparations,' Jeremy said after a few seconds of thought. 'Leave everything to me.'

Janet looked as though a great weight had suddenly been lifted from her mind. For the first time in days, she smiled openly. But behind the smile lay a mother's pride. 'Thank you,' she said simply.

Chapter Eighteen

Jardine reviewed the impressive frontage of the large, detached house with its professionally manicured lawns and trees. Even for this fashionable and expensive part of Edinburgh, the residence stood out as something special. Only a small brass plate fixed to one of the grey stone pillars supporting the wrought-iron gates betrayed the fact that the house served as anything other than a very exclusive private residence.

'Looks like Taggart wasn't so wrong after all,' Jardine muttered to Jackie Reid. 'There's certainly a call for psychiatrists in Edinburgh, if this place is anything to go by.'

'That's why people call them "shrinks",' Jackie put in. 'They specialise in shrinking people's bank balances.'

She pushed open one of the huge metal gates. 'Well, shall we go in?'

They walked up the long gravel drive towards the front door, which again bore a small brass plate. Jardine fingered the bell. In true Edinburgh fashion, the first few bars of 'Flower of Scotland' chimed out inside the house.

'Very nice,' Jackie murmured sarcastically. They both waited for a few moments until the door was opened.

Dr Miriam Daniels was a short, plump woman in her mid-fifties. She eyed her two visitors guardedly, making no move to invite them in.

'Dr Daniels? Detective Sergeant Jardine and DC Reid, from Maryhill Police Station, Glasgow,' Jardine announced. 'We telephoned you earlier this morning.'

Dr Daniels nodded, her face becoming slightly more welcoming. 'Oh yes, of course. Please come in.' Ushering them over the threshold, she showed them down the long hallway into an expensively furnished drawing-room. It did not boast a couch, Jackie noted.

Dr Daniels motioned for them to sit down in a couple of soft armchairs, making herself comfortable on a long quilted bench underneath the window. She regarded them both curiously.

'It's very good of you to see us at such short notice,' Jardine said. 'We'll try not to take up too much of your valuable time.'

Dr Daniels acknowledged the apology with a faint shrug. 'It's all right. As it happened, I had a cancellation.' She paused for a second. 'Now, as I understand it, you're interested in Marjory Helliwell – is that right?'

Jardine nodded. 'We were hoping you could give us some more information regarding the circumstances of her death,' he told the woman.

Dr Daniels frowned slightly. 'I can't imagine why the police would be interested after all these years,' she admitted. 'There is absolutely no question that it was a suicide, you realise that? It wasn't the first time she had attempted to kill herself.'

'We understand,' Jackie put in. 'This is really nothing to do with Marjory Helliwell's death, as such. More to do with her family, really.'

Dr Daniels was thoughtful for a while. 'Of course, you do realise that under normal circumstances such information would be protected by patient privilege.' she informed them. 'But since Mrs Helliwell is dead, and the case itself is so old, I suppose I can't see any harm.'

Jardine gave her a grateful smile. 'That's very good of you, Dr Daniels. We appreciate it,' he told her.

'So, what do you want to know?' the woman asked.

'Firstly, exactly why she killed herself,' Jardine responded.

Dr Daniels framed her thoughts, taking a deep breath. 'Marjory Helliwell was what we term a manic depressive,' she started. 'In layman's terms, that means that she had a deep-seated obsession which kept her virtually on the brink of self-destruction for most of her life. My job was to keep her from going over that edge. Eventually, of course, I failed.'

'This obsession – what caused it?' Jackie wanted to know.

'A family tragedy,' Dr Daniels said. 'The Helliwells had two children – a girl, and a younger boy. The girl,

Rhona, was diabetic. It was while they were living in South Africa that they lost their daughter. A young hospital doctor made a mistake and gave her an overdose of insulin. Rhona died, and all of Marjory Helliwell's problems stemmed from that tragic event.' Dr Daniels broke off, staring at Jardine with a sad look on her face. 'The combination of anger and grief – and guilt – can be a heady cocktail for anyone, and Marjorie was not a strong woman.'

'Guilt?' Jackie put in, seizing on the single word. 'How did she feel guilty about her daughter's death?'

'*Perceived* guilt,' Dr Daniels corrected. 'Marjory Helliwell convinced herself that she was at least partly to blame for Rhona's death by giving birth to a diabetic child in the first place. You have to realise that we are not dealing with a normal, rational mind here. The seeds of Marjory Helliwell's sickness were already sown at this point.'

Jardine nodded thoughtfully. He was beginning to understand. 'And you started treating her shortly after this? After the family returned to this country from South Africa?'

'That's right,' Dr Daniels agreed. 'They bought a farm near Penicuik and Marjory was referred to me after a series of depressive bouts. But there were already clear signs that her illness was much deeper than simple depression, of course.'

'What signs?' Jardine wanted to know.

Dr Daniels sighed. 'Marjory Helliwell became totally obsessed with the idea of having a daughter,' she went on after a while. 'It became such an irresistible force that she began dressing up her son in girl's clothes. She even gave him his sister's doll to play with and totally smothered him with protection. For almost two years, the boy was virtually a prisoner in the house. Eventually, the social services were called in and the boy was taken into care. This proved to be the breaking point for Marjory. Losing a second child was too much for her to cope with. She drowned herself in the farm pond.'

Jardine and Jackie were both silent for a long time after Dr Daniels finished recounting this harrowing family tragedy. Eventually, Jardine took it up again, realising that they had not even touched upon Malcolm Helliwell's part in the story. 'So what was Mr Helliwell's role in all this? What happened to him?' he asked.

Dr Daniels smiled thinly. 'Oh, he was really nothing more than a silent partner, in a way. He totally acquiesced to what his wife was doing just to keep the family together. A false sense of loyalty, if you like. Such things aren't uncommon in cases of child abuse.'

'Did he ever talk about getting revenge on the woman doctor who caused his daughter's death?' Jackie asked.

Dr Daniels flashed her a piercing, suspicious look, immediately on her guard. 'Now, how did you know it was a *woman* doctor?' she demanded.

'Because we know who she is,' Jackie said simply. There didn't appear to be any reason to go into any greater detail.

But it was enough for Dr Daniels to put two and two together and come to a conclusion. 'So that's what this is about,' she mused thoughtfully. 'You think Malcolm Helliwell might be responsible for some crime?'

Jardine nodded. There was no point in trying to deny it. 'We have reasonable grounds for suspicion, yes,' he confirmed.

'Then I'm very much afraid that you've wasted your time,' Dr Daniels said flatly. 'You obviously didn't know that Malcolm Helliwell has been dead for the last fourteen years.'

The news came as a body blow. Jardine could only gape at her. 'Dead?'

'Another suicide,' Dr Daniels expanded. 'The boy came home from school one afternoon and found him lying in his office. He'd taken a drug overdose. The coroner recorded an open verdict, but there was little doubt that he'd deliberately taken his own life.'

Jackie Reid was confused. 'But I thought you said the boy was taken into care?' she queried.

'That's right – but he was returned to his father after Marjory's death.' Dr Daniels paused with a rueful smile. 'Whether or not that was the right decision is not for me to say, but the authorities seemed to think it was at the time. The boy and his father were very close.'

Jardine was still trying to recover from the shock news. He pushed himself to his feet, uncertainly. 'Well, I suppose there's no point in us taking up any more of your time,' he muttered. 'Thanks for your help, anyway, Dr Daniels.'

The woman shrugged. 'As I said when you arrived – I couldn't understand why the police should be interested in the Helliwell case after all these years. It was a sad story, but somehow inevitable, I feel. When a family tries to shut itself away with tragedy, tragedy always follows. But it's closed now.'

It was a personal rather than a professional opinion, but she was probably right, Jardine thought. But there was just one loose end left hanging in the air. Jardine picked it up. 'By the way – what happened to the boy?' he asked.

Dr Daniels shook her head. 'I'm afraid I don't know. He was fostered out at the time, of course – but he'll be grown up now. He could be anywhere.' She rose from the window seat, escorting them towards the front door. Both Jardine and Jackie were silent as she showed them out. Jackie didn't speak until they reached the car.

'So that's the end of the trail, then? Taggart isn't going to be very pleased.'

Jardine looked glum. 'That's for sure. Still, at least we can get back to work for one boss again.'

'It's a pity, though,' Jackie observed. 'I mean, Taggart's theory sounded so plausible.' She was thoughtful for a while. 'Well, which one of us gets the job of breaking the news to him?' The resigned expression on her face suggested that she already knew the answer.

She was wrong. 'I'll do it,' Jardine offered, surprising her.

'You're a brave man, Michael Jardine,' Jackie told him, sounding quite impressed.

Jardine laughed. 'Not that brave. I'll tell him over the phone. That way he can bite the mouthpiece off the receiver instead of my head.'

They had reached the car. Jackie unlocked the door and reached in for the car phone. She handed it to Jardine. 'No time like the present,' she said, with a sweet smile.

Chapter Nineteen

The closure was official now. The majority of the guests had been filtering out of the building for most of the afternoon in what was a gradual retreat rather than a mass exodus.

Taggart's bags were packed, his blue tracksuit hung away in the wardrobe of his room – but he was in no hurry to leave. He had already stalled his departure for nearly two hours, generally wandering around and finding a succession of reasons for various trips to the toilet, the gym changing-rooms, or the guest lounge. A forgotten book here, a lost pair of plimsolls there, a few brief words of chat with one of the departing guests – Taggart was deliberately playing for time to be the last to leave, and using that time to watch, observe, and take mental notes.

For perhaps the fifth time during the afternoon, he sauntered casually through the reception area, on the pretext of studying the various brochures and pamphlets in the display rack near the reception desk.

Taggart's continued presence had not gone unnoticed. Behind the desk, Ian Gowrie glowered at him with barely repressed annoyance. 'Still here, Mr Taggart?' he muttered eventually.

Taggart slipped the brochure on aromatherapy which he had been reading back into the rack. He smiled disarmingly up at Gowrie. 'Waiting for someone to come and pick me up,' he lied. He sidled up to the desk. 'Looks like you're out of a job then,' he said, with a complete absence of tact.

The young man's face fell for a second, shortly to be replaced by a thin, almost sadistic smile. 'Oh, I've still got one little bit of unfinished business here,' he said, making it sound like a vague threat.

Taggart's ears pricked up. 'Oh, and what's that?'

Gowrie stared him straight in the eye. 'Getting guests to pay their final bills before they leave,' he said, pointedly.

It was Taggart's turn to glower. He'd walked right into the trap. With a sour face, he delved into his pocket and drew out his chequebook, spreading it out on the top of the desk. 'You'll not be charging me for this last day?' he muttered cannily.

Gowrie punched out Taggart's details on the automatic accounting machine, sliding the itemised print-out which it produced in Taggart's direction. He regarded the total morosely, taking scant comfort from the knowledge that a sea cruise from Aunt Hettie's legacy was now completely out of the question.

The reception telephone rang. Gowrie picked it up, his little rehearsed speech of apology ready on his lips. Recognising Jardine's voice, Taggart snatched the receiver out of Gowrie's hand. 'That'll be for me,' he said brusquely. Praying for encouraging news, Taggart held the telephone to his ear. 'Yes, Michael? Any news?' he asked optimistically.

Jardine's tone was instantly apologetic. 'Dead end, I'm afraid, sir. Malcolm Helliwell died fourteen years ago. Suicide.'

Taggart's face betrayed the depth of his disappointment. He was silent for some time. 'Well, that's it, then,' he muttered finally. 'It looks like I was wrong a second time.'

Grim-faced, Taggart handed the telephone back to Gowrie, who flashed him a triumphant, irritating smile. 'Having a bad day, Mr Taggart? I am so sorry.'

If looks could kill, Ian Gowrie would have expired on the spot. With a growl, Taggart finished writing out his cheque and stomped away from the reception desk in angry silence. He returned to his room, slamming the door behind him and gazing moodily at his bags ready-packed on the floor. They seemed symbolic, somehow – almost accusatory. Unfinished business, leaving before the job was done. A retreat. Taggart's frustration rose like a tight knot in his throat. There was nothing else he could do. With a heavy heart, he stooped to pick up his bags and carried them to the door.

Halfway along the corridor, Lavinia Jeffrey was also just carrying her suitcases out of her room. Taggart got the strangest feeling that she had somehow been waiting for that precise moment to leap out of hiding and waylay him.

She looked up, smiling coyly as he approached. 'Looks like we're the last two stragglers,' she observed. 'But I didn't want to leave without saying goodbye to you.'

Taggart forced a friendly smile. 'That's nice of you, Lavinia.' He dropped his own bags and moved towards her. 'Here, let me take your cases down to reception for you.'

The offer was gratefully accepted. 'Oh, I do like having a strong man around,' Lavinia cooed. She fell into step beside him as he hefted up her heavy cases and set off down the stairs.

Reaching the reception area, Taggart placed Lavinia's cases down on the floor beside the door and straightened up. They faced each other somewhat awkwardly, acquaintances rather than friends.

'So this is it, then,' Lavinia murmured, moving closer to him.

Taggart had the most unnerving feeling that she was about to embrace him. He took a nervous step back. 'Well, nice to have met you, Mrs Jeffrey . . . Lavinia,' he mumbled uncomfortably. He began to edge away towards the staircase to retrieve his own bags.

Lavinia followed him, trotting behind at his heels like a faithful puppy. 'Perhaps we'll meet again at some other health resort,' she suggested, as they climbed the stairs together.

'I rather doubt that,' Taggart mumbled, trying hard not to make it sound too much an expression of relief.

They had reached the top landing and Taggart's luggage. Lavinia gazed around the interior of the house fondly. 'It's a terrible shame,' she said sadly. 'I really loved coming to this place. Some of the regulars were like old friends. I shall miss it.'

Taggart paused in the act of stooping down to pick up his bags. He straightened up again, regarding Lavinia with renewed interest. 'Yes, of course – you knew most of the regulars here quite well, didn't you?'

Lavinia nodded, giving him one of her suggestive little smiles. 'And a few of their secrets,' she confided. 'You'd be amazed what people let out when they're naked in a sauna together. It sort of loosens the inhibitions, I suppose.'

'How well did you know Mrs Drake?' Taggart asked, feeling his way and trying to sound as casual as possible. He was aware that he was probably chasing candles in the wind, but it was just possible some vital snippet of evidence had been overlooked. And if anyone held such a snippet, it would be Lavinia Jeffrey.

Lavinia shrugged. 'Not what I'd call intimately. She was quite a secretive sort of woman, rather aloof. Funnily enough, the police asked me about her as well. Apparently it was someone pretending to be her that lured Dr Napier to his death. She was one of his patients, you know.'

'Oh, really?' Taggart feigned ignorance. 'I don't think I ever actually spoke to the woman.'

'I did point her out to you once,' Lavinia reminded him. 'She left a couple of days ago, shortly after all that nastiness with Belinda Napier's murder. The police asked me a lot of questions about her at the time.'

'And what did you tell them?' Taggart wanted to know.

Lavinia gave a guilty little smile. 'Actually, I lied and told them I didn't know her at all,' she admitted. 'I suppose that's what they call perjury, isn't it? Anyway, it seemed the simplest thing to do at the time. I gave a statement about a traffic accident years ago, and ended up spending two days in court giving evidence. It was simply frightful.'

'But you *do* know something about her – this Mrs Drake?' Taggart prompted, becoming a little impatient. He hadn't really intended to launch a full-scale gossip session.

'Oh yes, I learned quite a bit about her over the years,' Lavinia said. 'Little bits and pieces I picked up here and there, the odd snatch of conversation, things other people let slip. I never got too friendly with her myself because she was such a dreadful bore. Always lording it over everyone as though they were only there to be her servants. But I expect that's what comes of having lived in South Africa.'

Taggart was only half-listening, and this last piece of information was delivered in such a casual manner that he nearly missed its significance. But when it did register, he seized upon it eagerly. There it was again – the South African connection. It had to be more than just coincidence, something which Taggart was not a great believer in anyway. 'South Africa? Mrs Drake lived there?'

Lavinia nodded. 'For about fifteen years, I understand. Her second husband was a plantation owner. That's where all her money comes from. She sold up and came back here when he died eight years ago.'

Taggart found it hard to contain his rising sense of

excitement. 'Listen, Lavinia – you don't know exactly where in South Africa she lived, do you?'

Lavinia was staring at him with a rather puzzled expression on her face. She had never known Taggart to be such a keen conversationalist before. She shook her head. 'No, why – is it important?'

'Yes, it could be.' Taggart's face was suddenly stern and businesslike. The case was suddenly alive again, when it had appeared to be dead. And any lead, no matter how tenuous, had to be followed up. Even Taggart himself was not quite sure why this one was so important to him, why he was so loath to let it go. It had become almost an obsession. 'Try to think of any other details you can remember about Mrs Drake,' he urged, forcefully.

Lavinia's own expression hardened. She was seeing a new Jim Taggart – one she had never suspected. He was suddenly much less appealing. 'I have her address, if that's any help,' she offered, sounding a trifle wary. 'She gave it to me once, and I wrote it in my diary.'

Taggart produced a pen and a piece of paper from his pocket, handing it to her. 'If you wouldn't mind writing it down for me.'

Lavinia's eyes narrowed as she scribbled down the address. She regarded Taggart piercingly. 'Do you know you're beginning to sound just like a policeman?' she said, a little coldly.

Taggart grinned ruefully. 'I just wish I could begin to act like one.'

He didn't bother to explain further.

Chapter Twenty

The mansion house was dark and empty now, looking as though it could have been lifeless and derelict for years. The signs announcing that it had ever been a thriving health resort had all been taken down and stacked away in one of the outbuildings. The last guest room had been locked, the last window shutter closed against the buffeting winds and driving rain of another stormy night.

Jeremy Napier stepped through the front door into the cover of the porch, dragging a couple of suitcases behind him. Setting them down, he carefully locked the door, feeling a helpless sense of finality. It seemed strangely ironic that he had contributed so little towards keeping the place running over the years, yet it fell to him to perform this last, symbolic act of closure. He turned towards the driveway, where his mother and Gilbert Vance were exchanging their last goodbyes under the cover of a large golf umbrella.

Jeremy stared at them, illuminated in the head-lights of Vance's waiting car. They looked like lovers, he thought. Lovers about to part forever. The scene reminded him of the last few seconds of the film *Casablanca*. He tried to shake the bizarre thought from his head, but somehow it refused to be dislodged. It was as though it were there for a purpose, offering some sort of comfort against the many other turbulent and conflicting emo-tions which were swirling around inside his head.

Sadness prevailed over all. Sadness for his mother, who was saying goodbye to a dream. But beneath it lay a seething, bitter anger, a raging hate for the dark forces which had driven them to their present situation. And yet deeper beneath that, there was also a lurking sense of panic and desperation which threatened to rise above it all and engulf him completely. What was he to do now? Where could he go? What possible purpose could he find in his life now that the crutch which had been his sole support for so many years had been kicked away?

He stooped to pick up the suitcases and stepped out in the rain, walking towards his mother's car.

Janet Napier held Gilbert Vance's hand, lightly. 'I'm sorry it has to end this way, Gilbert,' she murmured sadly. 'You've been with us longer than anyone.'

Vance put on a brave smile. 'It seems good things never last, doesn't it?' he observed. The smile faded quickly, to be replaced with concern. 'What will you do now?'

'We're going up to the cottage for a few days,' Janet

188

told him. 'To rest, think, try to come to terms with what's happened. After that, maybe I'll start making plans – I just don't know.'

Vance nodded understandingly. 'Well, don't let any worries about this place add to your troubles. I'll drop by every few days to make sure everything's all right. At least until you make up your mind what to do, or until a new owner takes over.'

Janet squeezed his hand. 'That's sweet of you, Gilbert. Thank you. And thanks for staying to say goodbye.'

Vance looked surprised. 'Didn't everybody?'

Janet gave him a thin, sad smile. 'Oh, most of the staff were as understanding as they could be, under the circumstances. Nurse Clark popped in with a few words of sympathy, and most of the casual staff at least said goodbye on their way out. Everyone except Ian Gowrie, that is. I think he may have been too upset.'

A slight frown passed across Vance's forehead. 'Strange,' he muttered. 'He didn't say goodbye to me, either – and I don't recall actually seeing him leave.'

They both turned towards the mansion as a sudden flash of lightning threw the gothic façade into abrupt and eerie illumination. It looked like the archetypal haunted house, emphasising the oppressive sense of death which had taken over the place and turned a dream into a nightmare. Janet shivered briefly, turning her eyes away from the house. She looked up at Vance again. 'Well, goodbye, Gilbert – and thanks for everything,' she said simply.

Vance nodded, turning away towards his car. 'Goodbye – and good luck,' he called over his shoulder. He climbed into the car and drove off down the driveway.

Jeremy ran from the cover of the porch to join his mother under the umbrella, wrapping his arm around her shoulder. 'Come on, it's time for us to go too,' he murmured.

Janet looked up at him, taking comfort from his embrace. 'You're all I have left now,' she said wretchedly. Half-turning, she looked back at the darkened house again. 'Apart from my memories,' she added. The afterthought served to remind her that there was something she had forgotten. Something which was now of crucial importance in her life. She looked up at her son apologetically. 'Sorry, darling, but I have to go back in the house for a moment. Put the cases in the boot and get the car started, will you? I promise I won't be more than a minute.'

Thrusting the umbrella into his hand, Janet ran back to the house and opened the front door again. Making her way across the darkened reception lobby by instinct, she stooped down behind the desk and pulled down the power switch on the main fuse box. The lobby and stairway lights snapped on. Strangely, the sudden illumination seemed to emphasise the emptiness of the big house rather than diminish it.

Pausing only to switch on the upstairs-landing lights, Janet crossed to the stairway and began to climb the stairs. Reaching the top landing, she headed directly for the private living area and opened the drawing-room door. The room already looked like a mausoleum, all the furniture covered in huge white dust-sheets and every book, photograph, ornament or vase removed from the shelves.

With a sigh, Janet walked across the dark room without switching on the main light. She crossed to the bureau and writing desk that Gerald had always used for his private papers and stripped off the dust cover. Beneath it, there was a small anglepoise reading lamp lying on its side. Righting it, Janet switched it on and turned it round so that it cast a small pool of light on to the surface of the writing desk. She pulled open the top drawer.

It was there, as she had suddenly remembered it would be. Janet reached into the drawer and pulled out the thin photograph album that had been one of Gerald's most treasured possessions. Janet stroked the album's leather binding lightly, lovingly, feeling a sense of guilt. How could she have almost forgotten it? she asked herself. This book which contained all of their memories, everything they had been to each other.

Picking the album up, Janet held it against her heart for a few moments, a wave of emotion rising in her breast. It was all she had left of him now, the sum total of nearly thirty years of marriage and family life. Gently, she laid the album down on the desk and flipped it open at the first page.

How young they both seemed, Janet thought with a sense of wonder. No more than teenagers, it seemed. She gazed at the first photograph they had had taken together outside the hospital, remembering the tall, slim young doctor who had swept her off her feet with the power of his dreams. 'Someday I'm going to have my own clinic,' he had told her. 'Where anyone – rich or poor, black or white – can come and expect the same treatment, the same care.'

191

It hadn't happened, of course. Dreams get changed by circumstance, modified by the harsher realities of the real world. Janet wondered briefly if Gerald had ever regretted turning his back on South Africa to follow her home. Whether he had ever seen the health resort as little more than a poor compromise. If he had, then it was to his credit that he had never allowed her to know it.

She flipped over another couple of pages, gazing lovingly at the slightly browned and faded photos they contained: Gerald, looking like the great white hunter in his smart safari suit and bush cap; a picture of them both on the veranda of the game lodge they had stayed at on a trip to a game reserve; herself sitting on the lawn outside the pavilion of the East London cricket club watching her fiancé take five wickets in three overs.

Janet slammed the photo album closed again, suddenly remembering that Jeremy was waiting for her. She gathered up a few more loose photographs and papers which lay in the bottom of the drawer and turned to leave.

The room was suddenly plunged into inky blackness as the lights abruptly went out. Janet gave a little start of surprise before her body froze, her heart pumping wildly, her breath caught in her throat. The chill of fear crept over her slowly but inexorably, making every muscle in her body tighten and contract.

A peal of thunder cracked and splintered the night outside the house, causing the windows to rattle violently. The sound galvanised Janet into movement again, making her jump. Gerald's words sprang to her mind, unbidden. 'There's madness in the night.' The lights came on again, flickered once, and settled back to normal. Janet shuddered with relief, gathered the papers and photographs together in her arms and ran for the drawing-room door.

She hurried along the corridor and down the stairs to the reception area. It was only when she could pause there, steadying herself against the comforting solidity of the reception desk, that she allowed herself to start breathing normally again. She leaned back against the desk for some time, taking one last, sad look around the interior of the great house.

Then, drawing a deep breath, she stooped down to turn off the main power switch again and returned the house to pitch darkness. Hurriedly feeling her way along the edge of the desk, she made her way to the front door and let herself out of it for the last time.

The car was directly facing the front of the house, its engine running and the headlights on full beam, illuminating the porch like a stage set under a spotlight. Grateful for the light, but slightly dazzled by the intensity of the beam, Janet locked the front door and turned towards the waiting car, screwing her eyes up against the glare. Poising herself on the balls of her feet, she pulled the collar of her raincoat up over her head and jumped off the porch, making a run through the driving rain for the welcome shelter of the car. Reaching the passenger door, she threw it open and clambered in, slamming the door closed behind her.

At last daring to relax, she settled back into the plush upholstery, pulling down her raincoat and shaking the rain out of her hair with a toss of her head. She stared straight ahead out through the rain-lashed windscreen, trying to focus her eyes once again. 'Right, let's go,' she said to Jeremy.

There was no answer. Still slightly blinded by the glare of the headlights, Janet turned her head sideways to look at her son directly. He was strangely silent and immobile, sitting stiffly in the seat with his head lolling back against the headrest. He looked as though he had fallen asleep at the wheel.

'Jeremy?' Janet murmured, a puzzled catch in her voice. She reached out to prod him gently on the shoulder. 'Jeremy – wake up.' His head rolled gently sideways, to stare vacantly at her with open, but unseeing eyes. Janet's own eyes widened in sheer horror as they took in the great, bloody gash which had opened up his neck from just under his right ear to the base of his chin. Mute terror ripped through her body, making her shudder violently in her seat, rocking the whole car.

Jeremy's lifeless body began to slip sideways. Almost in slow-motion, he collapsed over her with his head laying in her lap and his blood seeping on to her clothes.

Janet Napier began to scream, as though she would never stop.

Chapter Twenty-One

Not for the first time in his career, Taggart found himself torn between his orders and his instincts. Perhaps if he could have remained at the health farm, he might have been able to sit it out for a few more days, taking some comfort from his continued, though vicarious, association with the Napier case through his contact with Jardine and Jackie Reid.

But now even that compromise option had been closed to him. With the shut-down, Taggart had been pushed into a reassessment of his position, and he found it untenable. Thrown out on the streets again, he felt like a eunuch in a harem. A street copper without a job to do. In fact nothing to do, except perhaps slink home with his tail between his legs like a runaway puppy. It was not a pleasant prospect.

Taggart sat in the snug bar of the city pub, where he had spent the last few hours brooding over three halves of bitter. Before that, it had been nearly two hours of wandering around aimlessly, desperately trying to force his brain into making a decision – any kind of a decision. All to no avail – he still felt as helpless and impotent as the moment he had stepped out over the threshold of the health resort that afternoon.

He took another unenjoyed sip from his glass, running the development of his theory through his head again for the umpteenth time. It always came out the same way; everything began, and appeared to end, with Malcolm Helliwell and the South African connection. It was the apparent incontrovertibility of this fact which contained the essence of Taggart's frustration. He had been so sure that his hunch was right, that the pieces could be made to fit. It had all seemed so promising. Even now, in the light of what he knew, that conviction remained firm in his head. His gut instincts screamed at him to follow it through, despite McVitie's dire warnings of what would happen if he interfered.

Taggart applied himself to this particular aspect of his problems. Perhaps it wasn't so much a question of what he *could* do as what he actually *should* do, Taggart agonised with himself. For given a reasonable lead to follow, he would have no compunction about risking McVitie's wrath by directly involving himself. He felt little doubt that he could justify such a course of action – if only to himself. His superior had ordered him to take a rest, and he had complied with that order. It was not Taggart's fault that the health clinic had closed down. So, technically at least, Taggart now considered himself back on duty. Morally, it was only a short step to convincing himself that he was, in effect, a free man again, having fully served out his time of penance.

His only problem, then, was in finding a duty to perform.

Having trained his thoughts along these lines, Taggart began to feel a little more optimistic. His mood improved noticeably as he realised he had somehow broken the sense of inertia which had been holding him in thrall. That was the negative aspect of his stay at the health farm, he thought to himself ruefully. He had spent the best part of a week getting his body into tiptop shape, but he had allowed his mind to become lazy. Now, having broken the deadlock, it was rapidly beginning to return to normal.

He could now review his options from a much more positive standpoint. McVitie ceased to have any relevance to the situation. Taggart had clashed directly with his superior on more than one occasion in the past, and would doubtless do so again several more times in the course of his career. In a way, such clashes went with the territory. And, anyway, they kept McVitie on his toes, Taggart reasoned further. He was probably doing the man a favour.

Taggart returned his full attention to the case in hand, knowing that things were much simpler now. He still had his original hunch, and no choice but to follow it through, despite an apparent dead-end. So, since there appeared to be no new avenues to explore, he was stuck with what he already had – the South African connection. And Mrs Drake was his sole remaining link to that connection.

Taggart glanced at his watch. It was just after eleven fifteen. Late, but perhaps not *too* late, he thought. He fished in his pocket, drawing out the slip of paper on which Lavinia Jeffrey had written down Mrs Drake's Glasgow address. It was less than a two-minute taxi ride away, he realised. Impulsively, Taggart jumped to his feet, having finally made the decision he had needed to make.

Chapter Twenty-Two

Janet Napier's screams had subsided now, to be replaced with great, wracking sobs which shook her body interspersed with animal-like whimpers. Terror was a numbing force, holding her locked in the car seat with the hot and sticky feel of her son's blood against her cold flesh. Her wide, frightened eyes stared blankly out through the windscreen of the car, into the blackness of the night, through the driving sheets of rain.

It was out there, the terror screamed in her head. The madness was out there in the night. Perhaps just feet away.

Perhaps to escape from it, perhaps even to confront it, Janet Napier returned to life again, her hand scrabbling frantically against the door handle. Finally throwing the door open, she slid herself away from the horror of her son's corpse and almost threw herself out of the car. She landed sprawled on the rain-soaked ground. Raising herself to her hands and knees she crouched there like a tormented beast for a few moments, still making the pathetic, animal-like noises in her throat.

Another flash of lightning threw the driveway into flickering illumination for a split second. Lifting her head into the sudden glare, Janet realised that there appeared to be nothing between herself and the gates – and beyond them lay the road, and her only hope.

Summoning every last ounce of will, she raised herself to her feet and began to run towards the gates, still sobbing hysterically. The driving rain stung her face, but she could not feel it. The wind blew her sodden hair over her eyes, but she didn't really have to see where she was going. Blindly, instinctively, she just threw herself down the driveway towards her sole chance of escape from the terror which lurked in the night.

She reached the huge metal gates, slamming her shoulder painfully against one of the heavy uprights as she rushed madly through. The force of the collision knocked her sideways, almost toppling her off her feet – but somehow she recovered herself and kept running, oblivious to everything except the fear which drove her.

She was out in the lane now, and running towards the road – splashing through the puddles and stumbling on the patches of uneven ground. One particularly deep pothole clutched at her foot like a grasping, ghostly hand. Janet fell headlong to the ground, scraping her hands and knees and smashing the air from her lungs.

Her fingernails ripped and tore into the mud and gravel of the lane as she fought to pull herself to her feet once more. Finally scrambling upright, she tried to run again, but could only manage an awkward, loping shuffle in which every movement brought an acute pain knifing through her chest.

She reached the junction and threw herself out into the middle of the country road. Pausing there, sobbing hysterically and gasping desperately for breath, she looked from side to side frantically, praying for the headlights of a car in the inky blackness. There was nothing – only a faint glow of light which came from beyond the trees where the road curved into a left-handed bend. It had to be the pub, Janet thought, and the realisation brought the faintest glimmerings of hope back to her. Turning in that direction, still in the middle of the road, she began to drag herself towards it.

She rounded the bend, now progressing at little more than a laboured, heavy lurch. The pub was in clear view now, perhaps a matter of fifty or sixty yards further down the road. The hanging sign outside was in darkness, and most of the pub's main lights were already switched off. But there was still a yellowish glow from the downstairs windows which told her it was not yet closed down completely for the night. Her relief lent her a renewed burst of hope and energy. Breaking into a slow and painful jog once again, she ate up each precious yard as her chance of sanctuary drew nearer.

The heavy oak door looked reassuringly solid and protective. Janet threw herself against it, pounding upon it with her clenched fists, screaming and sobbing with what breath she had left in her tortured lungs. 'Let me in, for God's sake, let me in,' she moaned frantically. She turned round, pressing her back and shoulders tighter against the door, as if the hard feel of it was protection in itself. Kicking against it with her heels, she gazed fearfully out into the blackness of the night, wondering from which direction the killer would come.

There were faint sounds of movement from within the pub, then came the reassuring rattle of heavy iron bolts being drawn back. The door opened, and Janet fell over the threshold to lie whimpering and sobbing on the floor. She gazed up at John through terror-filled eyes.

'Please – close the door. For God's sake, close the door,' she urged him, desperately. She scrabbled across the floor on her hands and knees, huddling up against the nearest wall and cringing there like something only partly human.

John shut the heavy door, slamming the double bolts back into place. He turned, walking across to her and reaching down to help her to her feet.

Janet accepted his strong arms gratefully, pulling herself upright and clinging to him like a drowning man would cling to a life-raft. She allowed him to guide her over towards the inglenook fireplace, where the last of the logs still blazed fiercely. 'Come on, Dr Napier. Just try to relax,' John muttered calmingly. 'Sit here by the fire. Try to pull yourself together.'

Janet sank down at the side of the fire, still clinging to his arm. She looked up at him pleadingly, desperately, realising that he could not possibly understand. Her terror for her own life was starting to subside now, but the horror of what had already happened was still with her.

She began to shiver uncontrollably, her whole body wracked with shuddering, neurotic spasms. 'Someone's killed Jeremy,' she managed to blurt out, through chattering teeth. 'Do you understand? There's a killer out there.'

John disengaged himself from her grip as gently as he could. He reached for a handy towel, thrusting it into her hands. 'Calm down, Dr Napier. You're safe now,' he assured her. 'The doors are all locked, no one can harm you in here. Now, dry yourself and try to pull yourself together and I'll go and phone the police.'

Janet took the towel and began to mop at her soaked hair, relief flooding into her at the realisation that she had made somebody else understand. Her shivering began to fade away as the heat from the blazing fire seeped into her chilled body. John took one last, concerned look at her to make sure she was calming down before turning away towards the bar and heading for the telephone in the passageway outside.

Seconds later, Janet heard the faint sound of numbers being dialled, and a longish pause before John started speaking. His voice was calm, but authoritative. 'Hello – can you give me the police? Yes, it is an emergency. My number is 339 6233.' There was another, much longer, pause as the operator transferred the emergency call. 'Hello – is that the police?' John went on at last. 'Yes, I want to report a murder, near Dr Napier's health farm. No, I didn't witness it myself, but I have Janet Napier here now. She says her son has been murdered, and she thinks the killer is still outside somewhere.'

Janet's head drooped with a combination of relief

and weariness as John rattled out the address. Help was on its way at last, she realised, but this thought was utterly swallowed up in the bitter knowledge that it came too late for her son.

'Yes, Dr Napier is perfectly safe here,' John was assuring the police. 'The whole place is locked and barred, and I'll stay with her. Only please hurry, will you?'

Janet heard the sound of the receiver being replaced in its cradle. John appeared back behind the bar, taking a glass and reaching up to the row of spirit optics. He poured a large glass of brandy and stepped out from behind the bar, carrying it across to her. 'Here, drink this,' John urged. 'It will help calm you down.' He took the towel from her hands, draping it carefully by the side of the fireplace to dry out again. He handed her the glass of brandy, which Janet accepted gratefully.

John returned behind the bar, leaving her to compose herself. Janet sipped at her glass, letting the fiery liquid burn out the last of the lurking cold within herself. After a while, she looked over towards John, her eyes helpless and hopeless. 'Why have they done this to my family?' she asked wretchedly. 'How much longer must this madness go on?'

John regarded her with a cool, level gaze. 'It won't be long now, Dr Napier,' he assured her. 'It will all be over soon.'

Janet stared at him without understanding for a moment. Then turning her head away, she dared to look out of the nearby window into the night again. Her eyes fell on a small child's chair which stood on a small ledge in the alcove of the window. Seated in it was a large, life-sized chocolate-coloured doll whose open, glassy eyes seemed to stare at her in mute accusation. It was an odd sight to find in a pub, Janet's confused mind registered vaguely. Questioning, she glanced back at John again.

He smiled at her without warmth. 'It will all be over soon,' he repeated, his voice oddly distant.

Chapter Twenty-Three

Cynthia Cunningham, Mrs Drake's housekeeper, opened the front door on a safety chain and peered out, regarding the bedraggled figure of Taggart somewhat guardedly.

He grinned at her sheepishly, feeling slightly guilty about the lateness of the hour. Fishing in his coat pocket, he produced his ID card for her inspection, brandishing it through the crack of the door. 'Detective Chief Inspector Taggart, Maryhill Police Station,' he announced. 'Look, I'm sorry to be calling so late, but it is vitally important that I speak to Mrs Drake.'

The housekeeper continued to eye him with suspicion for a few moments, before grudgingly slipping off the chain, opening the door a little wider and stepping back into the hall. 'Well, I suppose you'd better come in,' she muttered uncertainly. 'Luckily for you, Mrs Drake hasn't retired for the night yet.'

'Thanks.' Taggart stepped over the threshold, grateful to be out of the rain. He peeled off his wet coat, handing it to the woman to hang up for him. He followed her down the long hallway towards the drawing-room, where she brought him to an abrupt halt with an imperious wave of her finger.

'I'll just announce you,' she said formally. Leaving him standing there, she opened the double doors and stepped into the room. 'Oh, Mrs Drake – there's a Chief Inspector Taggart here to see you,' she announced. 'He says it's vital he talks to you.'

'Really? How utterly intriguing,' came the reply, delivered in a cultured, Borders country accent. 'Do show him in, Cynthia.'

Cynthia Cunningham backed out of the doors, ushering Taggart in and withdrawing discreetly.

He stepped into the lavishly furnished room, peering about a little uncertainly for a few seconds. It appeared to be empty. Then he noticed a thin plume of faintly blue smoke curling into the air from above the back of a high, wing-backed chair pulled up by the fireside. Taggart stepped forward, coming abreast of the chair. He recognised Mrs Drake at once. She looked almost exactly the same as the last time he had seen her, sitting alone in the pub near the health farm. The same dark glasses, the same silver cigarette holder with the Black Russian cigarette. Only one detail was different, and Taggart made mention of it, as much as for an ice-breaker as anything. 'No tracksuit,' he observed.

Any surprise that Mrs Drake felt at recognising him

in turn was masked by a thin smile. 'Escapees reunion?' she enquired, slightly sarcastically.

Taggart shifted his feet a little awkwardly. 'Not exactly,' he muttered. 'Look, I'm sorry to call on you this late . . .'

Mrs Drake dismissed his apology with a careless wave of her hand. 'No matter, Mr Taggart. I'm a bit of a night owl anyway. So, what is it you want to talk to me about? I suppose you realise that I have already spoken to Superintendent McVitie?'

Taggart nodded. 'I thought you would have.'

Mrs Drake gestured to another easy chair nearby. 'Please, do sit down,' she invited.

As Taggart sat down, she rose to her own feet, crossing the room to a well-stocked cocktail cabinet. 'Would you care for a drink, Chief Inspector? I'm going to have one.'

Taggart nodded. 'Thanks, I'll have a whisky, if I may.'

'You may indeed.' Mrs Drake poured him a healthy measure in a cut-glass tumbler, helping herself to a particularly large gin. Handing him his drink, she returned to the wing-back chair and sat down again, regarding him with a curious, almost amused look on her face. 'A most bizarre business,' she observed finally. 'A complete and utter mystery.'

Taggart eyed her over the top of his glass. 'Bizarre?'

'Why someone should want to impersonate me to lure poor Dr Napier to his death. As I pointed out to Superintendent McVitie yesterday.'

'Did you tell him you'd lived in South Africa, by the way?' Taggart wanted to know.

Mrs Drake shook her head. 'No. He didn't ask, and there didn't seem to be any reason to mention it. Why – is it important?'

Taggart shrugged. 'Possibly not. It's just that it seemed rather a coincidence.'

'I lived in King William's Town – it's quite near the coast,' Mrs Drake volunteered. 'My late husband was a wine grower.' She paused, a slightly mocking smile playing about her lips. 'Tell me, were you at the health farm under cover, Mr Taggart?'

'Under orders,' Taggart corrected. It was a partial truth, at least.

Mrs Drake smiled knowingly. 'I rather suspected as much. Mind you, I still think that pie and chips was perhaps bordering on sheer gluttony.'

Taggart wasn't prepared to admit to that one. 'It was certainly expensive,' he conceded ruefully, thinking about his contributions to the penalty box. 'A minor form of extortion, technically.'

Mrs Drake smiled thinly. 'A necessary evil, in my case. I have to have a couple of gins in the evening. Can't get to sleep without them. Besides, I know John, the landlord, from the old days.'

Taggart was still thinking about his forced benevolence. 'Aye, he certainly knew how to make escapees pay,' he muttered idly. He stiffened in his chair, suddenly aware of the significance of the words he had just uttered. He downed the remaining whisky in his glass at a gulp.

'Another one?' Mrs Drake asked politely, misinterpreting the gesture.

Taggart shook his head distractedly. 'No thanks,' he

grunted brusquely. His mind was racing.

'There's no penalty box here,' Mrs Drake started to point out.

Taggart cut her short. He jumped to his feet, facing her directly. 'You said you knew John from the old days. What old days?' he demanded.

Mrs Drake failed to understand Taggart's sudden excitement. 'He used to live near me as a boy in East London,' she murmured.

'East London?'

Mrs Drake nodded. 'Yes. It's near King William's Town. His parents emigrated to South Africa when he was quite young . . .' She broke off abruptly, regarding Taggart with a puzzled expression. He was suddenly and strangely agitated, pacing up and down the room with a worried frown creasing his craggy features. 'Is there something wrong, Chief Inspector?' she enquired solicitously.

But Taggart was already diving for her telephone, as the last piece of the puzzle fell into place.

Chapter Twenty-Four

Beneath the cover of the bar counter, John's fingertips caressed the cool, polished metal of the African throwing knife, stroking each one of its three smooth and shining blades in turn. It was such a beautiful weapon, he thought. Each razor-edged, wickedly curved and spiked blade was a metallic miracle of symmetry, a delicate but deadly tribute to its maker's craft and skill. Grasping the throwing handle, John lifted it gently, testing its perfectly balanced weight. It was a thing of precision, a perfect killing tool. With the familiar feel of it in his hand, John's heart surged with the savage joy of revenge. He glanced over to where Janet Napier sat beside the inglenook fireplace, her back turned to him and her head buried in her hands. She looked so vulnerable, so utterly unaware of her fate.

A thin, cruel smile flickered across John's face. It would be so easy to finish it all now, he realised. All he had to do was to lift his arm above the counter, raise his hand in the air – and with one flick of the wrist send death spinning across the room to end a lifetime of vendetta.

But no – not just yet. He had waited over twenty years for this moment, and was in no hurry now. It was a time to be savoured, not rushed. Besides, he wanted Janet Napier to know and understand when she finally came to atone for her crimes. He placed the knife gently back on the shelf underneath the bar, taking a step back from it.

Janet turned towards him, lifting her head. 'How long before the police get here?' she asked urgently. 'It seems ages since you phoned.' She wrung her hands together, shuddering again. A sob rose in her throat. 'My son is out there . . . and I can't go to him.'

There was something terribly, dreadfully wrong, Janet realised in a moment of chilling revelation. John was grinning at her, as though enjoying some intensely amusing and personal joke. The blazing fire at her back seemed suddenly to lose its heat as the chill of fear returned to her mind and body. Her eyes opened wide in sudden, terrifying doubt.

'You did ring the police – I heard you,' she muttered thickly. It was as if the statement was to reassure herself against the suspicion which had started to grow like a malignant tumour inside her brain.

John nodded, still grinning. 'Oh, aye – you heard me,' he confirmed. 'But you didn't *see* me, did you?' The grin faded from his face. He was serious now, and strangely calm. He spoke in a firm, but oddly distant voice. 'I lost my family too, you see,' he told Janet. 'One by one, they all died.' He nodded across towards the window alcove, where the doll sat staring at them both. 'The doll belonged to my sister,' John went on. 'She was murdered.'

The terrible nagging doubt in Janet Napier's mind was becoming a certainty now. Suddenly, a whole series of tiny, previously insignificant little things seemed to take on a more definite and sinister meaning. The doll had been dripping wet when she had first spotted it – as though it had been out in the rain. John's hair was damp too, she noticed now. She looked down at the towel which he had handed her when she first arrived. It was almost as if it had been ready for her, as though she was expected.

Janet's body tensed. She began to edge herself off the bench seat, away from the fire, preparing to jump to her feet and make a run for the door.

John moved quickly to snatch up the knife, still holding it beneath the level of the bar counter, out of her line of vision. Slowly, he moved along the bar towards the door, countering Janet's tentative moves, ready to block her. 'My mother and father were murdered too,' he went on in the same detached, distant voice. 'But slowly – over the years. Just as I was.'

Janet was on her feet now, staring directly in his direction but seeing past him to the bolted and locked door. The key was still in the lock, she noticed, the two heavy bolts engaged but not latched down, ready to be drawn again. She feinted slightly to one side, as though about to break into sudden movement. John edged to the very end of the counter, a matter of a few feet from the open flap which would give him free access to the open bar.

'I took this pub to be near you,' he said. 'Near you and your family. Just like you've been near to mine all my life.'

Janet's eyes darted towards the door again, seeing her last chance of escape. It was now or never, she realised.

The chance never came. Anticipating her, John stepped out from behind the bar, slowly raising his arm into the air. Janet stared in horrified fascination at the evil, murderous weapon in his hand. Like a helpless animal trapped by a snake, her eyes were transfixed by the way the flickering flames of the fire danced and glinted on the three gleaming, vicious blades. She cringed back into the inglenook fireplace, seeking some form of protection, but there was nothing. The heat of the fire was burning her legs, but Janet was oblivious to pain against the greater evil which confronted her.

'And now it's time to pay,' John muttered. Drawing back his arm, he launched the throwing knife into the air, aimed directly at her head.

Janet screamed once and dropped to her knees, throwing her hands up over her face and eyes. The action saved her – for the moment. The heavy, spinning knife whistled through the air across the bar, embedding itself with a dull thud deep into the solid, heat-scorched wooden beam above the fireplace. In the stunned silence which followed, all movement in the room was frozen for a few seconds, like a tableau.

Finally, John moved, running across to the fireplace and seizing the knife by its handle. One of the blades was embedded deep in the wood.

Grunting with exertion, John struggled to free it, jiggling the handle from side to side and tugging at it with all his strength. The knife refused to come free. It was stuck fast, held in a vice-like grip by the distorted, shrunken grain of the old oak.

She would never get another chance, Janet realised. Launching herself up from the floor, she threw the entire weight of her body against John's legs, just behind the knees. Obsessed with the problem of freeing the knife, and caught unawares, his legs buckled beneath him and he began to topple towards the fire. He fell headlong into the flames, his outstretched arm jamming between the bars of the heavy metal grate amongst the glowing, blazing logs.

Janet ran for the door, pulling back the heavy bolts as John's agonised screams filled the air. Without looking back, she threw the door open at last and fled into the night.

She ran blindly, with no sense of direction, aware only that she was following the line of the road. Her only thought was to put as much distance as possible between herself and the pub. She had no idea how much ground she had covered. One mile? Two? Finally, totally exhausted, she ground to a halt, her lungs almost bursting.

She turned round, staring back up the road in desperation, knowing that she could run no further. In the distance, the swathe of a car's headlights carved through the blackness of the night, heading towards her. She sobbed with relief, hardly daring to believe that safety might finally be hers. Janet stepped into the middle of the road to greet the approaching car, waving her arms frantically to attract the driver's attention.

It was an old Land Rover, Janet noticed, as the vehicle drew closer and began to slow down. She began to stagger towards it as it finally pulled to a halt.

The door opened, and the driver dropped down into the road. He was just a dark shadow behind the glare of the headlights, but Janet could see that it was a man, and he was moving towards her. Thankfully, gratefully, Janet took a few more dragging steps towards him as he drew nearer.

There was something odd about the way the man was moving, Janet realised suddenly. He had stepped beyond the headlights now, and she could see him more clearly. She froze in her tracks as the horror returned, hitting her like a savage blow in the gut.

Clearly in excruciating agony, John moved with the shambling, lurching gait of a drunken man. His badly burned arm steamed in the rain, his face was contorted with pain.

But behind the pain lay a look of savage, implacable determination. The face of a fanatic. John's insane hate had driven him for over twenty years, and it would not be appeased until the murderous quest he had embarked upon was finally over. It was a compulsion beyond reason, beyond understanding – beyond even pain.

Still frozen with fear and her own exhaustion, Janet could only stand and watch helplessly as he continued to stagger towards her, the evil throwing knife dangling from his burned and mutilated hand.

John lurched sideways, his knees buckling beneath him. For a moment, Janet thought he was going to fall, but then he seemed to right himself with a conscious effort and managed to take a few more shambling steps. He was obviously close to collapse, Janet realised, wondering whether he actually had the strength left to throw the knife. Or was he just playing a deadly game of cat and mouse with her – dragging out the final moments of her death for his own twisted, sadistic pleasure?

Either way, she could only continue to watch him moving inexorably towards her. Facing him gave her at least a slim chance of anticipating his moves, even perhaps avoiding the murderous weapon if he finally gathered up the will and the strength to launch it. She dare not turn her back to run, for that would present him with the advantage and the perfect target. She took a couple of slow, tentative steps backwards, her eyes firmly fixed on the knife in his hand, looking for the slightest suggestion of movement. It did not come. Emboldened, Janet moved back another two steps, and then two more. John continued to lurch forward, the throwing knife just dangling from his hand.

He stopped suddenly, bracing his feet slightly apart to steady himself. A cold shiver of premonition rippled through Janet's body. Was this the moment? She froze again, sensing that any further motion on her part would almost certainly precipitate his final move. Then, from behind her back, she heard the faint wail of police car sirens, getting louder and closer by the second.

John had heard them too, and in fact could already

see the fast approaching headlights and flashing blue lights now less than half a mile down the road. Slowly, concentrating every last ounce of mental reserve into fighting the agonising pain, he began to raise his injured arm into the air.

The wail of the two sirens was almost deafening now, and the entire scene thrown into brilliant illumination by the approaching headlights. The police cars had to be almost upon them now, Janet reasoned, still not daring to turn her head to check. Confirming this, she heard the sharp squeal of brakes, tyres skidding to a halt on the loose gravel of the country road and finally the sound of car doors opening and footsteps running towards her.

Jardine called out from behind her back. 'Drop the knife. It's over now.'

Only then did Janet dare to glance over her shoulder to look at him, and the two police cars slewed across the road behind him. With a deep, shuddering sob of relief, she began to turn to face him.

Jardine's eyes widened in sudden alarm, his mouth opening to yell out a warning. 'Look out,' he screamed at Janet. He exploded into action, jumping across the four or five feet which still separated them and tackling Janet in a shoulder-charge which took the two of them crashing to the side of the road in a tangled sprawl.

The knife, aimed at Janet's back, whistled through the air above them and embedded itself deep into the door panel of McVitie's car, just as he was climbing out, missing him by a matter of inches. To the man's credit, he hardly flinched. Pausing only for a split second to regard the still-quivering blades of the knife, he stepped out of the car and began to walk purposefully towards the prone figure of John, who had collapsed in the road.

Jardine clambered to his feet, lifting the distraught figure of Janet Napier up and huddling her in his arms. 'It's all over now,' he murmured, offering her what scant comfort he could.

Epilogue

'Good morning, sir,' Jackie Reid said chirpily, greeting Taggart as he strolled into the office.

Taggart grunted an acknowledgment, heading for his office.

'Feeling rested, sir?' Jardine asked.

Taggart's face was impassive. He wasn't giving anything away voluntarily. 'Yes, thanks. I can recommend it.'

Jardine dropped into step beside him. 'There's just one thing we don't quite understand, sir,' he muttered, speaking for himself and Jackie Reid. 'If you weren't an "escapee" yourself – then how did you meet John Helliwell?'

Taggart turned, flashing him a vaguely pitying look.

223

'Well, you didn't think I was there for the good of my health, did you?' he demanded. He turned away again, reaching for the handle of his office door.

'Oh, Jim,' McVitie called out, sticking his head out from his own office further up the corridor. 'Good to see you back.'

Taggart nodded. 'It's good to be back, sir.' He stood his ground, with his hand poised on the door handle, facing his superior in an open challenge, waiting.

McVitie's face creased into a grudging scowl, knowing that he was being put on the spot. 'Oh – and well done,' he muttered finally.

Taggart grinned at him. 'Thank you, sir. You know, sometimes you lose cases, sometimes you win them. And sometimes you just have to be philosophical about it.' With this parting shot, and a smirk of triumph, he ducked into his office and shut the door behind him.

Jackie Reid waited only for McVitie to close his own door before sticking her hand out under Jardine's nose, rubbing her thumb and finger together in an obvious gesture.

With a rueful smile, Jardine fished in his pocket and drew out a ten-pound note, handing it over. 'Some you win, some you lose,' he said, philosophically.